I0822288

SEAL

GHOST RECON

SEAL - Ghost Recon

This is a work of fiction. Names, characters, places, and incidents are products of the author's imagination or have been used fictitiously and are not to be construed as real. Any resemblance to persons, living or dead, actual events, locales, or organizations is coincidental.

ISBN: 979-8-9893424-1-9 (hardback)
979-8-9893424-0-2 (paperback)

Printed in the United States of America

GARY J. ROSE

DEDICATION

I'd like to express my heartfelt gratitude to my sister, Debbie (Rose) Miller, for her invaluable contribution to my manuscript as its first reader and editor. Writing involves imagination and creation, while editing demands interpretation and refinement.

Excelling at both tasks in isolation is already challenging, but excelling at both when working on the same book, especially one you've written yourself, feels nearly impossible.

Debbie has seamlessly stepped into the role once occupied by our beloved mom, who now watches over us from the heavens above.

OTHER BOOKS BY THE AUTHOR:

HORROR NOVELS

House on Haunted Hill – Resurrection

Beneath the Earth

The Tingler – Unleashed

Carnival of Lost Souls

JEANNIE LOOMIS THRILLER NOVELS

Ark of the Covenant – Raid on the Church of Our Lady Mary of Zion

Star Chamber

Forgotten Plans

The Fourth Reich

Time Game

Thin Blue Line

House of Special Purpose

Black Heart/Black Cell

The Phantom Train

Roller Coaster

Snow Angel

NON-FICTION

Hitting Rock Bottom

Inside the Walls

How to Create a Public-School Military Style Boot Camp

TO DARE:

To challenge; provoke to action, especially by asserting or implying that one lacks courage to accept the challenge.

If you accept a *dare*, you're probably trying to prove how brave you are.

WARNING!

In the dimly lit corners of our lives, in the hidden recesses of our desires, lies a peculiar fascination with the daring and the unknown. We, as humans, have an uncanny ability to push the boundaries of our own bravery, to test the limits of our courage, often spurred on by the sweet temptation of dares. But, my friends, let me remind you of a timeless truth: caution, in the face of such dares, is the sentinel of our safety.

For in our pursuit of thrills and the conquest of our deepest fears, we may find ourselves ensnared in the very traps we've set for our own amusement. In the shadows of recklessness, there lurks a dark and ominous presence, waiting patiently to teach us the most harrowing of lessons.

In this novel, we venture into a tale where "dares" are woven into the very fabric of destiny, where bravery is a double-edged sword, and where the line between reality and illusion blurs into an indistinct and terrifying abyss. This is a narrative forged in the spirit of those legendary storytellers who dared to tread where others feared to go—a tale for the intrepid and the cautious alike.

So, my fellow readers, through the corridors of the inexplicable, fasten your seatbelts and prepare to embark on a journey that will challenge the very essence of bravery itself. Welcome to "SEAL - Ghost Recon," where dares have consequences far beyond imagination, and where the pursuit of courage may lead one down a treacherous path, into the heart of the unknown.

CHAPTER ONE

As the ominous arrival of Halloween loomed just a few weeks away, Branigan's Bar underwent a magical transformation into a realm of eerie enchantment. The establishment had undergone a complete metamorphosis, adorned with holiday decorations that cast a spell of both eeriness and allure upon its patrons.

Plastic pumpkins, their hollow grins frozen in perpetual delight, served as whimsical décor and also as holders for the coveted beer nuts, temptingly placed on the bar to entice eager revelers. Glowing plastic skulls and orange and black crepe paper dangled from the ceiling, adding to the eerie atmosphere.

Every nook and cranny of the bar bore evidence of Halloween's spirited presence. Plates adorned with the iconic candy corn were thoughtfully positioned on each booth, their vibrant colors and sugary allure drawing the eye like a siren's call.

Sylvia, the industrious barmaid, donned an ensemble entirely shrouded in the color black. Her attire included a stylishly short skirt paired with a sophisticated low-cut blouse, a push up bra, and even sported elegant black net stockings. Remarkably, despite her age well beyond her 60s, it was as if all she needed was a tall, pointed black hat and a broom in hand to fully embody the classic witch archetype.

Sylvia's choice of clothing, while unconventional for someone of her age, carried a sense of timeless allure and confidence. The sleek, monochromatic attire accentuated her charisma, making her appear enigmatic and intriguing, almost as if she were a character from a bewitching tale. Her age-defying style blended seamlessly with the rest of the bar's ambiance, creating an atmosphere that felt both contemporary and evocative of mysticism.

One couldn't help but be captivated by Sylvia's distinctive appearance, which effortlessly combined elements of the modern and the mystical, casting a spell of fascination on those who frequented the establishment. Her black-clad elegance was a testament to her unique persona, proving that age is no barrier to embracing one's individuality and dressing in a way that reflects one's personality and spirit.

However, it wasn't just the tables and bar that had felt the touch of Halloween's magic. Meticulously crafted artificial cobwebs enshrouded many of the rarely frequented off-brand liquor bottles, casting them into shadowy obscurity and enhancing the eerie ambiance.

These spectral threads extended to the overhead lights, which, though seldom illuminated, now bore the weight of these ethereal traps, shimmering as they dangled from their chandeliers. In Branigan's Bar, Halloween had woven an intricate tapestry, beckoning all who dared to venture into its ghoulish embrace.

A kaleidoscope of music spanning decades, from the late 1960s to the contemporary sounds of 2023, emanated from the heart of Branigan's Bar. The source of this auditory time-travel was an aging jukebox, a relic from days gone by, now given a digital facelift. Its inner workings had been ingeniously replaced by a modern contraption that played a curated selection of songs meticulously programmed by the bar's owner.

The music, though perfectly calibrated, served as a harmonious backdrop, infusing the air with nostalgia and groove. It didn't assault the senses with excessive volume; instead, it embraced the patrons in a melodic embrace, allowing them to enjoy both the rhythms of the past and the lively banter of the present.

In the midst of this auditory tapestry, Ryan "Falcon" Foster, having indulged in more libations than prudence dictated, had become the life of the bar. Dressed in Desert Storm camouflage pants, a snug tan t-shirt, and an old military jacket, he earned himself the nickname "Rambo" from some.

His voice carried above the music but not so loudly as to drown out the surrounding conversations. He was, in essence, two sheets to the wind—a raconteur weaving tales and spinning yarns, filling the air with his spirited discourse, all while the jukebox whispered its timeless tunes.

In a room filled with a mix of patrons, it was an unspoken rule to tread lightly around Ryan "Falcon" Foster. Unlike most of his fellow special force's personnel, who carried their valor like a silent badge of honor, Foster was a stark exception. His demeanor exuded an unapologetic confidence, a sense of self-assuredness bordering on audacity.

As a highly decorated Navy SEAL sniper, Foster had earned his reputation on the battlefield, and he made sure everyone within earshot knew it. His tales of perilous missions and audacious feats flowed freely, a testament to his unwavering bravery. Most present tended to avoid his intense gaze, for to lock eyes with Foster was to unwittingly invite a challenge. You certainly didn't dare refer to his as Rambo.

In contrast to his fellow members of the elite fraternity, who preferred to let their actions speak for themselves, Foster took a different approach by narrating his valor in vivid and often elaborate detail. He embodied an unapologetic sense of bravado, willingly sharing his war stories that ranged from the most harrowing experiences to the most audaciously daring escapades.

In the midst of his storytelling, the room often played the role of a reluctant audience, offering polite nods or the occasional forced chuckle. Foster's presence served as a striking reminder that not all heroes wore a cloak of modesty; some, like him, proudly wore their valor as a badge of honor for all to witness.

To those who dared to lock eyes with him, it was as if they had unwittingly ensnared themselves in a web of storytelling. Once Foster's gaze had captured a willing listener, they were in for a prolonged, drawn-out reenactment of one of his missions, and the more gruesome and intense the details, the better.

If someone happened to hear the same story more than once, there was no need for concern, because Foster had an uncanny ability to reinvent his narratives seamlessly, never skipping a beat.

Foster's tales were like a tapestry of heroism interwoven with layers of drama and embellishment. He spun his stories with a flourish, skillfully weaving together fact and fiction to craft a narrative that was both captivating and larger than life. In his presence, listeners were transported to the heart of battle, experiencing the adrenaline, fear, and triumph of each mission as if they were right there with him. Whether you admired or questioned his approach, there was no denying that Foster's storytelling was a performance unlike any other, leaving an indelible mark on all who crossed his path.

Foster, with a sly grin and a gleam in his eye, relished the rapt attention of those gathered around him at the dimly lit bar tonight. His reputation as a storyteller was well-known among his friends and patrons, and tonight, he was determined to leave an indelible mark on their memories. With each tale, he wove a gruesome tapestry of his experiences in Afghanistan, pushing the boundaries of believability.

His voice took on a dark, hypnotic cadence as he described firefights that transformed into surreal bloodbaths, where bullets ripped through enemy combatants with bone-shattering force. He spared no detail, conjuring vivid images of gore and carnage. His tales of survival became increasingly macabre, filled with nightmarish scenarios where his enemies met gruesome fates.

As Foster spun his web of horror, he watched the faces of his audience, delighting in their reactions. Some gasped, their eyes widening in disbelief, while others exchanged uneasy glances. He could almost taste their shock and fascination, and he reveled in it, relishing the feeling of holding them captive with his grisly storytelling. Foster's stories were his way of asserting dominance, a reminder of his experiences in the darkest corners of the world. But beneath the bravado, a gnawing emptiness remained, a void he desperately sought to fill with the shock and awe of his tales.

CHAPTER TWO

Behind the gleaming bar counter, there stood Jamal Hassan, a man of profound wisdom and seasoned years. As the proprietor of this establishment, his presence commanded respect. His face was etched with the telltale lines of countless stories, each mark a testament to the many chapters of his life. His eyes, deep and penetrating, held a reservoir of knowledge that could only be accumulated through a lifetime of diverse experiences and hard-earned lessons.

Seated across from Hassan, was his friend Yassa Farid, a fellow Afghan. Like Hassan, Farid was a gentleman of age and experience, his demeanor equally resolute. With every word he spoke, his voice resonated with unwavering conviction. The ambiance of the room seemed to pause, as if acknowledging the gravity of the discourse unfolding between these two venerable men.

Farid never directly engaged in conversation with Foster and stood out for his refusal to engage in direct conversation with the former Navy SEAL. Instead, he communicated his deep disdain through a symphony of facial expressions. From his raised eyebrows and thinly pressed lips to the exasperated sighs he let escape at just the right moments, it was clear that Foster's self-aggrandizing tales did not sit well with this silent critic.

As Foster launched into another bombastic story, the man's eyes would roll heavenward, as if seeking divine intervention to spare him from the impending deluge of bravado. When Foster punctuated his tales with exaggerated gestures, the man would quiver in thinly veiled frustration. It was a performance of disdain conveyed without words, a silent protest against the ceaseless torrent of exaggerations and self-promotion. He would look at Hassan and saw that he too, did not hold Foster in high esteem.

In the absence of direct confrontation, the man's expressive face became a canvas for his inner monologue, a rolling commentary on Foster's arrogance. And while Foster may have been oblivious to the silent judgment, the entire bar watched with amusement as this silent critic used facial expressions to say what everyone else dared not utter aloud.

However, the tension in the air was not solely a product of their spirited discussion about their shared love for their new homeland, America. What simmered beneath the surface, fueling the fervor in their voices, was a shared disdain for Foster, the frequent patron of the establishment, known for his overt racism towards Arabs and his incessant, self-aggrandizing boasts.

Hassan and Farid's friendship had been tested time and again by Foster's derogatory remarks and insensitive comments about their heritage. Despite their best efforts to maintain composure and civility, Foster's bigotry and penchant for bragging had taken a toll on their patience.

With each eloquent point they made to each other, Hassan and Farid hoped to counteract the negative energy that Foster brought with him, subtly but firmly challenging his prejudice and arrogance.

In that moment, the polished bar counter bore witness to more than just a discussion; it bore witness to a silent resistance against intolerance and a reaffirmation of the enduring spirit of unity that had brought Hassan and Farid together, transcending the divisive rhetoric that threatened to undermine their shared love for their adopted homeland.

The debate, like many that had come before it, centered on the elusive definition of true bravery. Words were exchanged like verbal arrows, each participant staunchly defending their perspective. Hassan believed that courage was often quiet, an inner strength that emerged in the face of adversity, while Farid argued that it was in the overt display of valor that one's mettle truly shone.

Amidst this spirited discourse, Ryan "Falcon" Foster had settled into his role as provocateur. His arrogance, fortified by the spirits he'd imbibed, escalated with each passing moment. It wasn't enough for him to merely engage in the debate; he sought to dominate it.

With his chest puffed out with exaggerated pride, Foster challenged anyone within earshot to question his courage, a challenge that left no room for subtlety. Even Hassan, who had seen his fair share of bravery in his long years, was not immune to Foster's provocation.

With a brashness that left no room for diplomacy, Foster openly questioned Hassan's own courage, daring to label him a coward. A tense silence enveloped the room, casting a palpable tension over the bar. Foster's temerity had drawn a line in the sand, and it was clear that the evening's events were destined to take an unforeseen turn.

Hassan, his patience exhausted by Foster's relentless insults, cast a withering glare in the brash former SEAL's direction. He paused for a moment, his eyes locking onto Foster's, as if sizing up the very essence of the man before him. Silence took over the bar as heavy tension acted like a gathering storm.

In a voice laced with both challenge and a hint of sardonic amusement, Hassan addressed Foster, his words dripping with sarcasm, "Ah, my Navy SEAL friend, Mr. Falcon Foster, the paragon of bravery. I wonder, do you believe in ghosts? You know. Spirits that walk the earth."

Foster's bravado momentarily faltered as he was caught off guard by Hassan's unexpected proposition. The room seemed to hold its breath, waiting for Foster's response, for his answer held the key to an intriguing twist in the night's proceedings.

CHAPTER THREE

Foster's laughter reverberated through the bar, a mocking amusement dancing in his eyes. He shook his head with an air of disbelief, causing the remnants of his earlier libations to sway precariously in his glass. A stray droplet of drool dared to escape the corner of his mouth, and he wiped it away with a dismissive wave of his hand.

"What are you talking about?" Foster retorted, his voice heavy with skepticism. "You think I'm afraid of ghosts? I've created many of them on the battlefield." He chuckled, a note of condescension threading through the sound. "There are no such things as ghosts, or spirits, or even haunted houses," he declared with unwavering confidence, as if he were settling an indisputable fact.

The patrons in the bar exchanged knowing glances, some suppressing smirks while others observed the unfolding exchange with raised eyebrows. Foster's denial of the supernatural came as no surprise, given his reputation for bravado. Little did he know that the path he was about to embark upon would challenge the very foundation of his beliefs, leading him to confront a darkness far more profound than mere ghost stories.

Hassan's gaze briefly flicked to Farid, who nodded in agreement with the bartender's proposal, having known about it in advance. Hassan then fixed his steady gaze back on Foster, his voice carrying a challenge that hung in the air like an unspoken dare. "My SEAL friend," he began, "would you be willing to stay in a reported haunted house, say, for a prize of $25,000?"

Foster's initial response was an incredulous burst of laughter that echoed through the bar, capturing the attention of every patron within earshot. He assumed a demeanor of pure amusement, sharing the absurdity of the proposition with the entire establishment.

Turning to face the assembled audience, he addressed them with dramatic flair, gesturing grandly with his hands. "Did you hear this dare?" he exclaimed; his tone tinged with sarcasm. "The Arab is actually challenging me to stay in a 'haunted house'!" Foster couldn't resist using air quotes to emphasize his skepticism. "And," he continued, his voice dripping with theatrical disbelief, "he's even going to give me $25,000. Can you believe that?"

He pivoted back toward Hassan, fixing his gaze squarely on the bartender. "This is a joke, right?" Foster questioned, his skepticism still evident. "You want to give me $25,000 to play your stupid game? What, you want me to stay in a haunted house and battle your so-called ghosts?"

Hassan's response was measured and nonchalant as he continued to wipe down the bar. "Well, if you are afraid, we can call off the bet," he suggested, his tone devoid of challenge, as if the entire proposition were merely an idle offer, casually extended to test Foster's mettle.

Amidst the chorus of hushed conversations and clinking glasses, a faint smattering of laughter bubbled up from a few patrons within the bar. The sound of their amusement reached Foster's ears, prompting him to turn his head to pinpoint the source of the mirth. However, his quick survey of the room revealed nothing, as the chuckles seemed to emanate from a shadowy corner, shrouding the culprits in anonymity.

Undeterred, Foster pivoted back toward Hassan, his countenance now a mixture of mild irritation and continued skepticism. "You might as well give me the $25,000 now," he declared, his tone laced with unwavering conviction, "since, as I said, there are no spirits or ghosts haunting any damn houses." His proclamation carried an air of finality, as if he had decisively settled the matter beyond dispute.

Hassan merely offered a knowing smile in response, his eyes holding a hint of mystery that danced beneath the surface. Foster's boldness and unwavering skepticism had set the stage for a challenge that neither of them could have foreseen, one that would test the very limits of Foster's courage and reshape his perception of the supernatural.

Hassan's words hung in the air, their weighty implications demanding Foster's attention. His proposition had been clear, and he awaited Foster's response with the patience of experience. "I will take that as an acceptance then," Hassan continued, his tone resolute. "If you can return here in three days, I will provide you with the address of the house. There is one condition, though." He paused, his gaze unyielding. "You must enter the house before the sun goes down and remain inside until the first light of sunrise. Is that acceptable to you?"

Rather than offering a direct answer, Foster chose to address the entire bar once more, his voice filled with a mixture of theatrical enthusiasm and a hint of bravado. "Okay, listen up, everyone!" he proclaimed, commanding the attention of the patrons who had been drawn into the unfolding drama. "You will be my witnesses. This Arab," Foster emphasized the word with flair, "has dared me to stay one night in a house of his choosing, from sunset to sunrise, and in exchange, he's willing to part with a cool $25,000." His words sparked a mixture of curiosity and skepticism among the assembled audience.

However, Hassan's response was swift, his voice carrying a note of exasperation as he corrected Foster's interpretation. "No, my SEAL friend," he interjected, his tone firm as he fixed Foster with a penetrating gaze. "That is not what I mean. You must not only stay one night in the house; you must survive it." His words hung like a spectral veil over the conversation, leaving an ominous chill in their wake as the gravity of the challenge became abundantly clear.

Foster's response was laced with dismissiveness. "Whatever," he retorted, his tone tinged with impatience. "I'll be back here in three days, and I expect that address ready for me. If you fail to deliver, remember, you'll still owe me that $25,000." His words served as a lingering reminder that the challenge had been accepted, and the stakes had been set.

CHAPTER FOUR

Three days drifted by like a slow-moving tide, and Foster's return to Branigan's was as punctual as it was expected. His swaggering demeanor remained unaltered, a reflection of his unwavering self-assuredness. Still wearing his military clothing, he approached Hassan. It was clear that very little conversation had transpired between the two during his three-day absence. Their exchange was characterized by the weight of unspoken challenges and the arrogance that clung to Foster like a second skin.

Hassan, with an air of stoic resolve, handed Foster a small piece of paper—the precious address that held the key to the night's impending ordeal. He also gave him the key to the front door of the house. Foster accepted both with a casual glance, his eyes briefly flickering to meet Hassan's, as if gauging the depth of his challenge. With a knowing smile that seemed to say, "This will be a walk in the park," Foster headed towards the exit.

"My SEAL friend, I must tell you that there is no need to take a cell phone with you, nor any other type of electronics. There has not been any power to the house in many years."

Before stepping out into the cool evening, Foster couldn't resist one final declaration, his voice rich with the same arrogance that had marked his demeanor throughout. "Was that supposed to scare me, Arab? Just have the $25,000 ready for me tomorrow morning, Arab," he proclaimed, his words a blend of expectation and bravado. It was as though he believed that the impending trial held no true challenge for a seasoned Navy SEAL like himself.

Initially, as Foster followed the GPS's erratic directions, he couldn't shake the suspicion that his trusty device was playing tricks on him. It seemed insistent on leading him up into the ominous hills that loomed over the city, a place that held little more than whispered legends of old, and nothing more, to his knowledge. Yet, the persistent virtual navigator's voice urged him onward, and so he ascended, his doubts mingling with a sense of curiosity that gnawed at his resolve.

Nearly twenty minutes of winding roads later, Foster's doubts crystallized into disbelief as he found himself standing before a structure that defied the passage of time. The disrepair of the looming edifice was starkly evident, its three-story height shrouded in an aura of sinister grandeur.

It was a gothic mansion, the likes of which could have sprung from the darkest recesses of the most unsettling tales. Its spires and bell towers pierced the sky like skeletal fingers, and the façade, adorned with ornate yet weather-beaten traceries, seemed to mock the very concept of decay. A long-abandoned fountain with gargoyles guarding the structure was located in the front.

The mansion's windows, mostly shattered or boarded up, gaped like empty eye sockets, bearing witness to years of neglect. Ivy, ancient and withered, clawed at the walls, entwining itself with the remnants of forgotten vines. The stone steps leading to the front entrance were uneven and cracked, as if bearing the weight of countless foreboding footsteps. Moss and lichen clung to the masonry, painting the dwelling in a palette of eerie greens and grays.

As Foster gazed up at this grotesque marvel, he couldn't help but wonder if this was indeed the house that Hassan had selected for his harrowing night. It was as if time itself had surrendered to the darkness that enveloped this place, leaving it trapped in an eternal twilight of decaying beauty and forgotten horrors. Foster's heart quickened, and a shiver ran down his spine as he contemplated the challenges that lay ahead in this macabre and forbidding abode.

To regain his confidence, Foster parked his truck in front of the looming gothic mansion. The shadowy presence of the house seemed to mock his bravado, urging him to summon the strength he'd so readily flaunted back at the bar. Determined to face the looming night ahead, he opened his duffle bag, which sat dutifully on the passenger seat, and began a methodical inventory of its contents.

His fingers wrapped around the cold steel of several Bowie knives, their sleek and deadly forms serving as a stark reminder of his military background. Foster knew that, even in the face of the supernatural, these weapons could provide a modicum of comfort and security.

Next, he inspected his prized Sig Sauer P226 9mm semi-autos, two formidable sidearms that had been his trusted companions in countless missions. Their weight in his hands was a reassuring presence, a tangible link to his past as a Navy SEAL.

His fingers brushed against the matte finish of a Benelli M4 Tactical Defensive shotgun; a potent firearm capable of unleashing a hail of destruction if needed. Foster's confidence surged as he took in the stockpile of ammunition, enough to face whatever unknown horrors might lie in wait within the foreboding mansion.

In addition to his arsenal, he discovered a cache of essential supplies. Several flashlights, their beams of light a beacon against the encroaching darkness, were tucked away neatly. Foster knew that these would prove invaluable as he navigated the uncharted territories of the house's interior.

A box of matches, each stick a promise of warmth and light, provided a small comfort against the pervasive chill that seemed to seep from the very walls of the mansion.

Lastly, Foster's fingers closed around a humble but essential sustenance—a sandwich he'd picked up from Subway on the way, practical fuel for his body and his resolve. And, to help him stay awake through the long night that lay ahead, a thermos of steaming hot coffee, the fragrant aroma of the brew serving as a steadfast companion in the lonely hours of the dark.

As he surveyed his arsenal and supplies, Foster felt a flicker of renewed determination. Armed not only with weapons but also the trappings of human survival, he was ready to confront the unknown horrors that awaited him within the house.

Exiting his truck, Foster carried the bulk of his gear in a sturdy duffle bag slung over his shoulders. He leaned casually against the vehicle, taking a moment to appraise the imposing structure that loomed before him. It was a substantial house, and as he studied it, a shiver of unease flickered through his thoughts. Was it merely his imagination, or had he just witnessed a flurry of bats taking flight from one of the ornate bell towers? The sight sent a ripple of trepidation down his spine.

Somewhere in the distance, the haunting caws of crows echoed through the air, adding to the eerie atmosphere that surrounded him. Foster couldn't help but comment to his companion, Arab, who had chosen this unsettling location for their endeavor. With a hint of dark humor, Foster said out loud to no one present, "I must say, Arab, even the master of horror himself, Stephen King, would be envious of the house you've selected for your game. It's almost reminiscent of the infamous Rose Red."

CHAPTER FIVE

Amidst the pitch-black night, Foster's approach to the foreboding structure was only sporadically illuminated by the jagged streaks of lightning that tore through the sky. Each flash briefly revealed the eerie outline of the house, its decaying facade taking on a nightmarish quality in those fleeting moments of illumination. Rain fell in relentless sheets, adding an extra layer of dread to the scene as he stood before the ominous mansion.

With his heart pounding and the thunderclaps echoing through the air, Foster felt an undeniable sense of foreboding that threatened to overwhelm him. The relentless storm seemed to conspire with the dilapidated house, amplifying the tension that clung to the night.

He fumbled in his pocket for his flashlight, his fingers trembling with a mix of excitement and trepidation. As the lightning provided another brief glimpse of the front door, he quickly found the aged key and inserted it into the rusty lock. With a reluctant groan, the door swung open, revealing a yawning darkness within.

With only the intermittent flashes of lightning and beam from his flashlight to guide him, Foster stepped over the threshold, his flashlight cutting through the obscurity with a narrow beam of feeble light. The entrance hall loomed before him, its vastness still shrouded in mystery. The staircase, cloaked in shadows, seemed to beckon him upward with its spectral fingers.

Foster's cockiness, once unyielding, now faced a formidable adversary in the form of the haunted mansion. The unsettling ambiance of the dark, cold house pressed down upon him with each step he took deeper into the abyss. His boasts of courage wavered as he realized that the true test of his mettle awaited him in the shadows ahead.

Determined to prove himself, Foster clenched his flashlight tightly, maneuvered his duffle bag on his shoulder, and ventured further into the house, his conceitedness warring with the heavy sense of dread that clung to the air. The storm raged outside, echoing the turmoil within him, and as he delved deeper into the darkness, he could only hope that his confidence would see him through the horrors that lay ahead.

At the foot of the grand staircase, which, like the rest of the house, was veiled in a sinister shroud of cobwebs, Foster paused to clear away the layers of dust and debris. With a swift exhalation, he brushed aside the accumulated filth on a table and gingerly set down his duffle bag, which carried the few supplies he thought he might need for the night's challenge.

As he bent down to open the bag, the ancient front door, bearing the weight of countless years of abandonment, suddenly slammed shut with a deafening, echoing thud. Startled, Foster's instincts kicked into high gear, and in a swift, fluid motion, he drew his trusty Sig Sauer from its holster, his senses heightened to a razor's edge.

The silence that followed was oppressive, the only sound being the rain pelting against the windows and the relentless howl of the wind. Foster's heart hammered in his chest as he scanned the entrance hall, his flashlight beam cutting through the suffocating darkness. But there was no sign of an intruder, no human presence to explain the door's abrupt closure. The dust on the floor only showed the footsteps he had left in his entrance into the house.

Foster, his nerves on edge, took cautious steps toward the door, his firearm trained on the ominous portal. He reached out with a trembling hand, fingers grasping the ornate doorknob, and tried to turn it. It remained resolutely locked, refusing to budge.

Panic gnawed at the edges of his composure as he fumbled for the key in his pocket, his mind racing to make sense of the inexplicable. But when he attempted to insert the key into the door's mechanism, a chill ran down his spine. There was no keyhole on the inside of the door, as if the very concept of escape had been intentionally removed.

A sense of isolation and dread washed over Foster, his bravery now but a distant memory. He was trapped within the malevolent confines of the haunted house, and the true horrors that lay hidden within its walls were beginning to reveal themselves. With every passing second, the house seemed to tighten its grip on him, and Foster could only hope that his Navy SEAL training would be enough to confront the sinister forces that now held him captive.

With a forced sense of swagger, Foster slid his trusty Sig Sauer back into its holster, the cold metal against his skin offering little comfort. In the dim light of his flashlight, his face contorted into a defiant scowl. He was determined to dismiss the unnerving incident as a mere trick of the house, placed by his tormentor, a futile attempt to rattle his nerves.

"Well played, Arab," Foster spat out with a strained grin, his voice quivering ever so slightly. "But you'll have to do better than that to scare me. You are the coward, not me!" His words echoed through the cavernous room, seemingly absorbed by the oppressive darkness that enveloped him, as if the very walls were listening. "Okay ghosts. Come out, come out, wherever you are." His invitation echoed throughout the vastness of the house.

Foster's shotgun made a resounding thud as he set it down on a nearby table, the weight of his weapon symbolizing the gravity of the situation. It was a moment that thrust his bravery into the spotlight once again. While he had confronted enemy fire in far-off lands, this was an entirely different kind of battle—one that dared to probe the depths of his own courage and test his mettle in unfamiliar ways.

As he stood there, the memory of Stephen King's Rose Red film began to play tricks on his mind. A wistful smile graced Foster's lips as he contemplated how the recollection of that movie had started to blur with reality.

In his humble opinion, Stephen King's novel "Rose Red" stood as one of the author's most masterful works, a literary gem that had left a profound impression on him. And when it came to its cinematic adaptation, the film soared to the zenith of horror cinema, nestling comfortably among the genre's finest.

A professor who had transitioned from the world of psychology to the enigmatic realm of parapsychology was at the heart of this eerie tale, and her audacious mission was to unlock the secrets of a purportedly haunted house known as the "dead cell."

With the blessing of the enigmatic mansion looming before them, a diverse group of individuals, each wielding their unique psychic abilities, converged upon its ominous threshold. Their journey, reminiscent of the very house in which our protagonist now found himself, would be one of profound discovery and dread.

As the group embarked on their exploration of the vast estate, much like the very mansion he had been dared to spend a night in, the sprawling edifice came to life in ways that defied reality itself. It underwent a haunting metamorphosis, its once-static facade unraveling into an intricate tapestry of rooms, each concealing its own dark secrets.

Like a never-ending maze of malevolent design, the mansion's endless corridors led them further into a realm of supernatural uncertainty, where the boundaries between the living and the dead blurred with each passing step.

But what lay at the heart of this enigmatic transformation? Was it the latent energy of the house, awakening in response to the psychics' presence? Or was there something more sinister, an evil force lurking within the mansion's walls, eager to ensnare the unsuspecting souls who dared to trespass on its domain?

The answers, like the mansion itself, remained shrouded in a miasma of chilling uncertainty, awaiting discovery by those brave enough to venture deeper into the heart of Rose Red.

If only he had more time, he mused, he might have delved into the depths of the Internet to uncover additional details about this mysterious mansion. Who were its previous owners? What dark and intriguing stories lay buried within the house's history? Maybe the damn house was built over an ancient Indian burial ground?" he laughed.

The questions swirled in his mind, taunting him like specters in the night. Foster's thirst for knowledge and his fascination with the enigmatic mansion's past urged him to embark on a quest for answers. He realized that this new challenge was more than just a physical test—it was a mental and emotional journey into the unknown, where the past and present converged in a tapestry of mysteries waiting to be unraveled.

In this moment, as he contemplated the shadows of the house and the secrets it held, Foster found himself drawn deeper into the intriguing narrative of the house, prepared to confront not only its physical challenges but also the enigma of its past.

Foster shifted his focus to a well-worn thermos that had seen its share of adventures. With a satisfying twist of the lid, he released the subtle but inviting aroma of freshly brewed coffee, a simple pleasure that offered a momentary solace amidst the foreboding atmosphere that enveloped him. The familiar scent wafted through the air, carrying with it a sense of reassurance and familiarity.

Gently pouring a cup of the steaming brew, Foster took a deliberate sip. The warmth of the coffee provided a comforting contrast to the pervasive chill that seemed to penetrate his very bones, as if the old mansion had a way of seeping into his very soul.

As he savored each sip, Foster found that the simple act of nourishing his body with this familiar elixir had a calming effect on his nerves. It was as if the rich, earthy flavors of the coffee served as a temporary shield against the unsettling ambiance that surrounded him. The reassuring ritual of sipping the hot beverage acted as a lifeline, grounding him in the present moment and reminding him that even in the face of the unknown, there were small comforts to be found.

In the quiet solitude of the mansion, Foster's coffee break became more than just a means to satisfy his thirst; it became a brief respite, a moment of reflection, and a source of inner strength. It was a reminder that sometimes, in the midst of uncertainty, the simple act of nourishing oneself could provide a sense of stability and calm, allowing him to face whatever mysteries lay ahead with renewed determination and resolve.

CHAPTER SIX

As Foster pressed on, the steady beam of his flashlight sliced through the oppressive darkness of the mansion, uncovering a haunting tableau of forgotten grandeur. The interior, much like the eerie house in Stephen King's Rose Red, appeared as a time capsule frozen in a bygone era. Glimpses of faded wallpaper, adorned with intricate patterns that had long lost their vibrancy, adorned the walls like ghostly memories of a once-vibrant past.

His flashlight's revealing light cast an unsettling glow upon aged furniture that sat beneath tattered, dusty sheets. Tables, chairs, and ornate cabinets stood like silent sentinels, their surfaces obscured by the passage of time. The sheets, once pristine, had grown threadbare and discolored, bearing the weight of forgotten decades.

In the ever-elongating room, Foster's steps echoed through the emptiness, a haunting reminder of his solitude in this vast, desolate space. The mansion seemed to stretch into infinity, its corridors and chambers intertwining in a labyrinthine fashion. It was as if time itself had woven a web of shadows and secrets within these walls, concealing stories that begged to be unearthed.

Each flicker of his flashlight unveiled another layer of the mansion's mystery, revealing the intricate beauty and melancholic decay that coexisted within its walls. The oppressive darkness and the spectral ambiance that clung to the mansion whispered tales of a history long forgotten, and Foster, guided by his unyielding curiosity, ventured further into the heart of this enigmatic place, determined to unlock the mysteries that lay hidden in its depths.

"I must admit, Hassan," Foster began, his words laced with a hint of sarcasm, "I'm rather taken with your choice of decor. It's like stepping onto the eerie sets of those classic Vincent Price horror films, you know the ones. House on Haunted Hill, House of Usher, the Pit and the Pendulum." He couldn't help but let out a nervous chuckle as he surveyed the ominous surroundings.

Foster's gaze lingered on the ornate yet decaying details that adorned the room, remnants of an opulent past now swallowed by the relentless march of time. His flashlight's beam danced over the faded wallpaper, revealing peeling edges that hinted at the years of neglect that had befallen the mansion.

He continued, “It’s quite a masterpiece, Hassan. But tell me, did it cost you a pretty penny to maintain this haunted charm?” His attempt at humor was punctuated by the uneasy feeling that the house held secrets far more terrifying than any film could capture. The atmosphere in the room seemed to thicken with each passing moment, and Foster couldn’t help but wonder if the price paid for this macabre beauty was far steeper than mere dollars and cents.

Despite his attempts to convince himself that he was in control, Foster couldn’t shake the feeling that he was not alone. The house held secrets far darker than any he had encountered in his military career, and it was now demanding that he confront his deepest fears.

As he stood there, coffee cup in hand and flashlight at the ready, he couldn’t help but wonder if the challenge he had accepted was not just a test of bravery but a descent into a nightmarish abyss from which there might be no escape. The true horrors of the haunted house were beginning to close in around him, and his defiant shout of courage had only served to further awaken the malevolent forces that lurked in the shadows.

CHAPTER SEVEN

With unwavering determination, Foster decided it was time to embark on his reconnaissance of the supposed haunted house. He reached for the shotgun resting on the table, feeling its cold, reassuring weight in his hands. He placed extra shells in his jacket pocket. The familiar metal of his Sig Sauers, holstered on his shoulder and one on his hip, provided additional comfort, like old friends who had seen him through countless battles.

Gripping the flashlight tightly in one hand, Foster descended deeper into the ominous darkness. Every step echoed with nervous energy, as if the very house itself was watching his every move. Cobwebs brushed against his face like spectral fingers, and the floorboards beneath his feet groaned in protest, as though resentful of his intrusion. He decided to first focus on the main floor before exploring the floors above.

The first room he entered was a relic of forgotten elegance, the remnants of grandeur now twisted into something unsettling. Moonlight filtered through cracked windows, casting eerie patterns on the peeling wallpaper. Antique furniture, draped in tattered sheets, seemed to conceal secrets of their own. The air hung heavy with a musty stench, a miasma of time and decay. The presence of mildew could be seen on the walls with a heavy concentration at their base.

Foster's breaths came in short, nervous bursts, and beads of sweat formed on his forehead. Each corner of the room concealed shadows that threatened to swallow him whole. He moved cautiously, his flashlight revealing faded portraits of unknown faces on the walls, their eyes seeming to follow his every step.

As Foster's mind wandered through the labyrinthine corridors of the mansion, thoughts of Stephen King's Rose Red resurfaced again like a haunting specter. He couldn't help but wonder if he had made a grave oversight by not bringing a length of rope with him, a makeshift trail of breadcrumbs to navigate the intricate web of rooms and passageways within this colossal structure. The idea of leaving a tangible path behind him seemed like a prudent strategy now, a lifeline to ensure he could find his way back amidst the mansion's bewildering complexity.

In the haunting narrative of "Rose Red," the mansion's ghostly transformations were as unpredictable as they were terrifying. As the house stirred to life, its eerie manifestations introduced a chilling element of uncertainty for the group of psychics and explorers who ventured within its foreboding walls. One of their precautions, a tether to a sturdy banister, became a lifeline between the living and the unknown.

The hallway they had confidently traversed would abruptly vanish, swallowed by the malevolent will of the mansion itself. This once-familiar passageway, which had been their only connection to the world they knew, would now be transformed into an ethereal barrier, a spectral wall erected by unseen hands, determined to entrap those who dared to tread too deeply into the house's dark secrets.

The group's members soon realized that the rope, once a simple precautionary measure, had become their salvation. Each step forward was tinged with trepidation, for they never knew when the mansion would conspire to change its layout once more. The very architecture of the house seemed to twist and contort, as if controlled by a malevolent intelligence, reshaping itself into a nightmarish labyrinth designed to ensnare and confuse.

Rooms, too, were subject to the whims of the supernatural. They morphed and shifted, their interiors reshaping like the volatile moods of a capricious phantom. It was a maddening dance with the unknown, where even the most familiar spaces could become traps, where the boundaries between reality and the supernatural were blurred beyond recognition.

With every uncharted corner, they ventured deeper into the heart of Rose Red, clinging to their lifeline of rope, their only anchor in a world where the very essence of the house defied reason and sanity. The mansion, like a ghostly architect, continued to reshape the boundaries of their understanding, forcing them to confront not only their deepest fears but also the inexhaustible depths of the unknown.

Regret coursed through him as he contemplated the missed opportunity. The notion of trailing a simple cord behind him felt like a missed chance to thwart the oppressive darkness and the ominous uncertainty that clung to every corner. But, as he sighed inwardly, he knew it was too late to rectify his oversight. He checked his wristwatch which also contained a compass. This will have to do, he thought.

In this ever-expanding maze of a mansion, Foster was left to rely on his wits and instincts alone. With each step he took further into the heart of the structure, the weight of his decision not to leave a trail of breadcrumbs pressed upon him. It was a decision that now served as a haunting reminder of his vulnerability and the unforgiving nature of the place he had ventured into.

Nevertheless, his determination remained unwavering, and with each step forward, he steeled himself for the challenges that lay ahead, knowing that in the absence of a lifeline, he would have to rely on his resourcefulness and courage to navigate the secrets and shadows that awaited him in the depths of the mansion.

As he explored further, the silence was broken only by the distant rumble of thunder and the relentless patter of rain on the windows. Every inch of the house seemed to conspire against him, and his cockiness now felt like a fragile façade. The true horrors that lurked within the mansion's depths remained shrouded in darkness, waiting for the opportune moment to reveal themselves to the unwelcome intruder. Foster couldn't shake the unsettling sensation that he was not alone, that something evil-minded watched and waited, ready to challenge his very existence.

His bravery surged within him as he meticulously continued to comb through the various rooms on the first floor of the mansion, uncovering nothing but a disconcerting pattern. "What's the matter, Hassan? Couldn't afford to get some ghosts to haunt your little house?" he shouted, not expecting and answer. He switched the shotgun to his right hand and continued.

It was as if an interior decorator had painstakingly crafted each room to mirror the others in almost every detail. The uncanny resemblance between the chambers only heightened the eerie atmosphere, intensifying the sense of disorientation that had settled upon him. It reminded him of trying to maneuver through a house of mirrors in a funhouse.

As he continued his exploration, Foster couldn't help but unleash a touch of humor in the face of the house's apparent lack of supernatural activity. With a wry grin, he called out to his friend, Hassan, the owner of this enigmatic establishment.

"Where are your spirits, Hassan?" His voice echoed through the seemingly endless corridors, filling the space with a sense of both jest and anticipation. "You might want to ask for a refund. No ghosts. No eerie organ music. Hell, I haven't even witnessed a crashing chandelier."

His words echoed in the air for a moment, a lighthearted challenge to the mysteries that the mansion was rumored to harbor. It was as if Foster was playfully daring the spirits to reveal themselves, confident in his skepticism.

Yet, beneath his jest, a flicker of uncertainty remained, for even the bravest of souls could not entirely dismiss the foreboding aura that clung to the mansion's shadowy recesses. In this strange dance between skepticism and apprehension, Foster ventured deeper into the heart of the mansion, determined to uncover the truth hidden within its walls.

Foster cautiously started his ascent up the creaking staircase was abruptly halted by a sound that sent shivers racing down his spine—a hideous, guttural male laughter. The laughter seemed to emanate from the very walls of the house, echoing through the desolate corridors like a sinister chorus. His heart pounded in his chest, drowning out the relentless storm outside.

Foster spun around in the room, clutching the shotgun with trembling hands, desperate to locate the source of the ghastly laughter. But the sinister laugh appeared to come from below, as though mocking his every move from the depths of the house. A realization crept over him; there must be a basement in this place, a shadowy abyss concealed beneath the mansion's decaying facade.

He remained on the first floor while his flashlight's beam darted across the room, seeking an escape from the encroaching terror. Finally, his gaze settled upon a door, its handle beckoning ominously. Without hesitation, he reached for the cold, rusted handle and discovered, to his unease, that it was unlocked. The metallic squeal of the hinges filled the room as he swung the door open, revealing a gaping maw of darkness that seemed to swallow all sound and light.

With the shotgun cradled firmly in his grasp, Foster aimed his flashlight down the steep, staircase that led into the menacing depths below. But just as the beam began its descent into the abyss, the flashlight abruptly flickered and died, plunging him into an oppressive blackness.

Panic welled up within him, and he pounded the flashlight's base in desperation, but it remained lifeless. Forced to abandon it, Foster retreated to the table on the first floor at the base of the stairs, where his trembling hands found a larger flashlight that still held power. It was as if the house itself had determined his path, leading him further into its terrifying depths.

Armed once more with a flickering beam of light and the weight of the shotgun in his hands, Foster began his descent into the unknown darkness below, his heart heavy with foreboding. The laughter continued to haunt him, echoing through the subterranean passageways, and he couldn't shake the feeling that he was descending into a nightmare from which there might be no escape.

With every cautious step down the dimly lit staircase, Foster's heart pounded in his chest like a relentless drum of dread. He moved slowly, every footfall an agonizing whisper against the ancient wood. Occasionally, he halted his descent, his trembling hand gripping the shotgun as he aimed the flashlight into the abyss below. Shadows danced and swirled in the cold, damp air, as if they were alive with evil intent. He constantly brushed cobwebs aside while others already captured his face before he could react.

Three-quarters of the way down, just as the oppressive darkness seemed to constrict around him like a tightening noose, disaster struck. The staircase, ravaged by years of neglect, betrayed him. With a sickening groan, a rotted step crumbled beneath his weight, sending him hurtling into the unforgiving embrace of the concrete floor below. His body slammed into the ground with a deafening thud, pain searing through his skull as he struck his head with brutal force.

The world around him swirled and distorted, the edges of his vision blurring as he gasped for breath. The flashlight, which had been his feeble lifeline, skittered away from his grasp, casting erratic beams of light that danced across the room, revealing nothing but a nightmarish tableau of decay and ruin.

As consciousness ebbed away, Foster's last lucid thought was one of paralyzing terror. He was now trapped in the heart of this venomous house, battered and disoriented, with the chilling laughter still echoing through the corridors. The darkness closed in around him, and he knew that whatever horrors awaited in this accursed place were now poised to seize him in their merciless grip. At least the hideous laughter stopped.

Time slipped away like an elusive phantom as Foster lay unconscious in the oppressive darkness. With his wristwatch's face shattered from the fall, he had no way of gauging just how long he had been out cold. As his senses gradually returned, he instinctively began to check his own vitals, his trained instincts taking over. A wave of relief washed over him as he realized that, aside from a throbbing headache and a sizable bump on his head, there were no broken bones or debilitating injuries.

With a deep, steadying breath, Foster slowly pushed himself upright, the world spinning around him as he fought to regain his balance. The headache pulsed with an agonizing rhythm, a constant reminder of his fall into this abyss. In the midst of his disorientation, he was determined to retrieve his flashlight and the shotgun he had clung to, as if they were his last lifelines in this nightmarish place.

Reaching out into the darkness, Foster's fingers brushed against the metallic body of his flashlight. He retrieved it with trembling hands and, guided by its faint beam, began his search for the shotgun. His fingers finally closed around the familiar stock, and the moment it settled into his grasp, a renewed sense of bravery coursed through him. The laughter returned as if to mock him and his fall.

Clutching the shotgun tightly, he couldn't help but vent his frustration into the suffocating darkness. "I should sue your ass, Hassan," he muttered bitterly, his voice echoing through the cavernous room. "You didn't tell me that damn place was a death trap." His bravado was back, albeit laced with a newfound edge of apprehension. With every step he took deeper into the sinister abyss, he couldn't shake the feeling that he was now in a fight for his life.

CHAPTER EIGHT

The ghastly laughter, more terrifying than ever, continued with a vengeance, echoing through the house like a sinister symphony of torment. This time, the sinister sound seemed to originate from the floor above, drawing Foster's attention away from his descent into the basement's abyss.

Determined, he began to ascend the staircase that led to the second floor, his footsteps deliberate and slow, each one resonating with trepidation. The creaking steps seemed to mock his presence, a cacophony of dread that reverberated through the decaying mansion. His head throbbed with each corresponding step.

As Foster reached the top of the stairs, his flashlight's beam pierced the darkness, revealing a chilling sight. At the pinnacle of the staircase stood a spectral, ghostly presence, its white form hovering in eerie defiance of the laws of the living. It seemed to gaze down upon him, its body translucent, allowing Foster to make out the faded, peeling wallpaper behind the apparition.

For a moment, Foster's boldness wavered, and he couldn't suppress the surge of fear that coursed through his veins. "Who the hell are you?" he shouted, his voice laced with a mixture of anger and terror. His trembling hands raised the shotgun in a defensive posture, the barrel aimed at the otherworldly intruder.

But in a macabre twist of reality, the figure before him dissolved into thin air, vanishing into the oppressive darkness of the house. Foster's breaths came in ragged gasps as he was left alone once more, his flashlight casting stark, erratic beams that danced wildly through the room. The apparition had been a chilling reminder that the horrors lurking within the haunted mansion were far beyond the realm of the living, and his grasp on reality was growing ever more tenuous with each encounter.

The second floor of the mansion stretched before Foster, a maze of numerous rooms cloaked in shadows and uncertainty. With apprehension trepidation, he mumbled to himself, his voice barely above a whisper, "This is going to take some time." It was a statement, not an invitation for dialogue, and yet, in this malignant place, he couldn't help but feel the chilling sensation that something unseen might be listening. A glance at his watch showed a smashed face and damaged compass. He concentrated on the various walls using the staircase for his bearing and then proceeded.

To Foster's astonishment, the first room he ventured into offered an unexpected sanctuary from the unrelenting decay that seemed to pervade the rest of the house. The sight that greeted him was truly surprising—a grand, oversized bed stood at the center of the room, bathed in a soft, ethereal glow. This magnificent piece of furniture was a stark contrast to the mansion's general dilapidation, and it exuded an aura of regal splendor.

The bed's headboard, towering against the wall, was a work of art in itself. Carved from heavy wood, it exhibited intricate patterns and designs that hinted at meticulous craftsmanship. The rich grains of the wood, which could have been stained oak, mahogany, or cherry wood, glistened under the faint illumination, casting an opulent and inviting ambiance throughout the room.

In this unexpected respite, Foster found himself drawn to the sumptuous bedding that was devoid of the suffocating presence of spiderwebs or dust. It was as if this oasis had been preserved in time, a haven untouched by the mansion's relentless decay. The sheets and blankets beckoned with their crispness, promising a night of comfort and solace.

Standing in the doorway, Foster marveled at the grandeur of the oversized bed, a testament to the mansion's enigmatic blend of opulence and abandonment. It was a fleeting moment of respite, a stark reminder that even in the heart of darkness, there were pockets of unexpected beauty and tranquility waiting to be discovered. With a sense of both wonder and caution, he approached the inviting bed, contemplating the mysteries that lay beneath its luxurious surface.

"Ah, this is better," he muttered with a hint of defiance. "I need a quick nap, Arab, to get rid of this damn headache, and then I'll be ready to continue your game."

With a sense of temporary relief, Foster leaned his shotgun against a nearby wall, trusting in the false comfort of the room. In one hand, he clutched the Sig Sauer, his fingers gripping it as if it were a lifeline to sanity. He patted the bed and was surprised that no dust rose from his impact. He lifted up the pillow and found no insects. As he lay down on the bed, exhaustion began to weigh heavily upon him. His head still throbbed. He closed his eyes, intending to steal a few moments of rest, but an unsettling intuition gnawed at him.

Before Foster could sink into the embrace of sleep, a strange sensation washed over him. His eyes snapped open, and he peered up at the canopy above, his vision still blurred from the lingering effects of his headache. Slowly, with an unsettling deliberation, he realized that the canopy was descending, inching ever closer to the bed. He had not noticed grooved in the four-poster bed that allowed the canopy to decent with ease.

Fear gripped him as he scrambled to sit up, but it was too late. Metal bars erupted from the mattress like nightmarish tendrils, wrapping around his body with an iron grip, rendering him utterly helpless. Panic surged through him as he realized that escape had been snatched away, and the very bed he had sought refuge in had become a nightmarish trap.

Desperation clawed at Foster's throat as he struggled against his macabre restraints, his mind racing with terror. The house had become an entity unto itself, an evil force that toyed with him at every turn, and he could only hope that he had the strength to endure the horrors yet to come. The canopy came closer and closer to steal his breath. He began to chock due to lack of oxygen.

Abruptly, Foster jolted awake, his heart racing in his chest, and his body drenched in the clammy aftermath of night sweats. The terror that had gripped him seemed to have released its hold. He glanced around the room, his eyes darting from the sweat-soaked pillow to the empty, untangled bed sheets. The constraints that had held him captive in the night were gone, as if they had never existed. He grabbed one of the posters that supported the canopy and found no grooves.

Slowly, his breathing steadied, and he reluctantly tore his gaze away from the bed, his eyes fixating on the canopy above. It was exactly where it should be, undisturbed and hanging innocently over the bed. The mattress beneath him felt reassuringly solid, devoid of the sinister apparitions that had haunted his sleep.

"Damn nightmare," Foster muttered bitterly, his voice quivering with the remnants of fear. He swung his legs over the side of the bed, his bare feet making contact with the cold, wooden floor. His gaze remained fixed on the canopy and the mattress, as if expecting them to betray him once more. The room, bathed in a pallid, moonlit glow, offered no answers, only the lingering echoes of his own dread.

As he stood there, still trembling from the vivid horrors of his dream, Foster couldn't shake the unsettling feeling that the nightmare was to continue. Somewhere the Arab was laughing his damn head off. He looked under the bed with his flashlight. There were no bars.

CHAPTER NINE

He slowly descended the stairs and reentered the kitchen. Remarkable, he noticed that the laughter had stopped. Finally, some peace, he said to himself. He started to grab his thermos when the deafening roar of AK-47s erupted from the floor above. Their rapid bursts of gunfire shattering the fragile calm that had briefly settled over the house.

Foster's heart hammered in his chest as he instinctively grabbed his shotgun, his breaths coming in ragged gasps. Panic surged through him as he sought refuge beneath the kitchen table, a flimsy shield against the chaotic storm unfolding just overhead.

In a maddening crescendo, the AK-47s' staccato gunfire was met with the thunderous response of M16s, their reports blending into a cacophony of violence that reverberated through the mansion's walls. The once quiet and shadowy corners of the house now bore witness to a ferocious battle, where the echoes of conflict intermixed with the lingering malevolence that seemed to seep from every crevice. The kitchen had turned into the landscape he recognized: Afghanistan, the Bora-Bora tunnel system.

Then, as suddenly as the tumult had begun, silence descended upon the vast house like a mausoleum. The landscape turned back to the familiar kitchen. The abrupt cessation of gunfire left Foster trembling, sweat trickling down his cheeks as he lay sprawled on the cold kitchen floor. The lingering taste of terror was noticeable, a bitter reminder that the mansion was a battleground, a twisted arena where forces beyond his comprehension clashed in a terrifying symphony of violence.

Summoning every ounce of courage, Foster slowly rose from his shelter beneath the table, his shotgun cradled in trembling hands at the ready. His senses were on high alert, but the eerie silence that enveloped the house now felt even more oppressive than the chaos that had preceded it. He knew that whatever sinister forces were at play, they were not done with their nightmarish game, and he braced himself for the horrors that lay in wait, lurking just beyond the edges of his vision.

Foster's patience had worn thin, like a fragile thread stretched to its limits by the relentless tension of the night. He stood firm, his voice carrying a mixture of exhaustion and determination. He called out the house. "Enough is enough, Arab," he proclaimed, his words cutting through the eerie silence that clung to the mansion's darkened corners. "I'm tired of your damn games. Let's put an end to this so I can finally collect my hard-earned $25,000." His words echoed through the vastness of the mansion like he and his fellow warriors witnessed as they went from one tunnel to another in the mountains of Afghanistan.

The room bore witness to his resolve as Foster swiftly gathered all of his equipment, packing it meticulously into his well-worn duffle bag at the base of the stairs. The bag, heavy with the tools of his trade and the weight of the unknown, slung over his shoulder like a shield. With a fresh flashlight in hand, its beam cutting through the oppressive shadows that seemed to recoil from its light, Foster readied himself for another ascent into the heart of darkness.

Each step he took on the creaking wooden stairs reverberated with determination. The staircase, a once-grand architectural feature, now served as a sinister conduit to the upper reaches of the house. The second and third floors loomed ahead, shrouded in an unsettling stillness that was anything but comforting. The laughter had now been replaced with groaning and occasional female screams, as if a person or persons were undergoing torture. His attention focused on any repeat appearance of the ghostly apparition seen previously.

As Foster climbed, he could feel the noticeable weight of the house's evil pressing down upon him.

The promise of the $25,000 prize was a beacon, a reminder of the purpose that fueled his resolve. Yet, the mansion held secrets far more chilling than he had ever anticipated, and he knew that confronting those horrors was the only path to redemption. With each step, he inched closer to the unknown, guided only by the flickering beam of his flashlight and the unwavering determination to face whatever darkness lay ahead.

Foster's determination surged as the laughter replaced the groaning and grew louder with each step, drawing him closer to a room he had not explored before. The air itself seemed to vibrate with hostility, a chilling resonance that sent shivers down his spine. He approached the door with hesitation, his fresh flashlight's beam cutting through the surrounding darkness as if it were a beacon of defiance.

With a slow, cautious motion, he turned the knob and began to push the door open. However, as the door widened, an uncanny phenomenon occurred. The room seemed to possess a voracious hunger, greedily absorbing the flashlight's light, swallowing it whole as if the very darkness itself were alive and hungry. The encroaching void threatened to consume everything that attempted to enter, leaving Foster in a disconcerting half-light, teetering on the precipice of the unknown.

As he stepped further into the room, the door behind him suddenly slammed shut with a thunderous force, reverberating through the chamber. Panic surged within Foster as he frantically tried to grasp the doorknob, but it refused to yield to his desperate attempts. He was trapped.

In the blink of an eye, the room transformed before his disbelieving eyes. The chilling laughter had given way to an entirely different kind of chaos. The once-vacant space had become a battlefield, one that Foster recognized all too well. It was Kamdesh in Afghanistan, the scene of past horrors he had hoped to leave behind.

Without hesitation, Foster dropped to the ground, his instincts taking over as he retrieved his trusty Sig Sauer. The room erupted in a tempest of flashes and deafening gunfire, with bullets flying in all directions. American and Arabian words were thrown about. Foster fired back into the chaotic fray, the sound of his weapon echoing in the confined space. The battle seemed to stretch on for an eternity, an unrelenting onslaught of enemy fire, the air thick with the acrid scent of gunpowder. He replaced his first clip with a second and then a third.

Then, as abruptly as it had begun, the battlefield vanished into the void, leaving Foster gasping for breath in the oppressive darkness. His flashlight's beam revealed an empty room, devoid of the war-torn battleground that had manifested so vividly just moments before. His expended shells scattered on the floor gleaming when hit by his flashlight. He saw holes in the walls from his handgun which he confirmed by putting his fingers in them.

He inspected four walls however, and only found evidence of his shooting. There were not marks from other projectiles nor any damage from grenades and RPG that he witnessed.

Panic and confusion washed over him as he struggled to make sense of the impossible. The room had played host to a nightmarish apparition, a ghostly reenactment of past traumas. The devilish forces at work in the house had revealed a glimpse of their true power, and Foster couldn't help but fear what other horrors lay in store as he continued his harrowing journey through the haunted depths of the house.

Attempting in vain to rationalize the harrowing ordeal that had just unfolded, Foster's mind reeled, struggling to find a foothold in the maelstrom of terror. His thoughts were a fractured mosaic of disbelief and horror, each shard a reminder of the inexplicable horrors he had witnessed. But his futile introspection was abruptly shattered by a chilling sound.

From the floor above, a haunting melody echoed through the mansion, its eerie notes cascading like an avalanche of despair. It was the unmistakable sound of an organ, but there was nothing harmonious about it. The music had no structure, no rhythm, as if the unseen person at the keyboard were simply slamming their hands upon the keys in a frenzied, discordant frenzy.

Foster's fingers instinctively found the holster of his Sig Sauer, but he hesitated, the shotgun now held firmly in his grip. With a heavy swallow, he holstered the handgun, preferring the firepower and reliability of the shotgun in this treacherous environment. Whatever awaited him on the third floor demanded a different kind of preparation.

With each step, the oppressive weight of the house pressed down upon him, as if the very walls themselves were conspiring to keep their secrets hidden. The staircase led him upward, toward the uncharted territory of the third floor, where the sinister music continued to reverberate like a dirge for the damned.

As he ascended the staircase, the dissonant chords of the organ music grew louder, their disharmony a haunting soundtrack to his journey into the darkness. Each step brought him closer to the source of this phantom symphony, and he couldn't help but wonder what horrors lay in wait on this unexplored level of the mansion. Thunder and lightning outside grew in their intensity as if daring him to continue on.

The battle-hardened Navy SEAL was about to face a terror unlike any he had encountered before, and he steeled himself for the relentless horrors that awaited him on the third floor.

CHAPTER TEN

With a heavy breath, Foster pushed open the door to the third-floor room, and he stepped into an eerie tableau that sent a cold shudder through him. The dim light revealed a male figure hunched over an old-fashioned organ, attired in unmistakably traditional Afghani dress – a perahan tunban, a light jacket, a tunic shirt, loose pants, and a head covering that concealed their features in shadow. The room seemed suspended in time, offering a haunting glimpse into a world from the distant past.

The figure paid no heed to Foster's entrance, as if unaware of his presence in the room. Instead, its hands continued to slam down upon the organ's keyboard with a frenetic and discordant rhythm, creating a sound of madness, an unholy symphony that filled the air with a ghostly aura. It pounded on the organ keyboard the way a young child would do fascinated in its ability to create noise with no concept of tone or melody.

Foster's pulse quickened as he observed the mysterious figure's relentless assault on the keyboard. The room itself appeared to be untouched by the ravages of time, as if it existed in a realm outside the confines of reality. The discordant music hung in the air, a haunting refrain that seemed to seep into his very soul.

He couldn't discern the figure's intentions, nor could he fathom the significance of this eerie encounter. But one thing was certain – the room held a presence that defied explanation, a ghostly performance that defied the laws of both time and reason. As Foster stood there, a profound sense of unease settled over him, and he couldn't shake the feeling that this encounter was just another piece of the chilling puzzle that was the mansion's dark and enigmatic history.

At times it appeared that the figure timed his slamming on the keyboard to the sound of the thunder outside, but then again continued to slam away with no connection.

In the eerie stillness of the room, time seemed to stretch and contort as the ghostly apparition slowly pivoted to face Foster. His heart raced, and he held his shotgun steady, his nerves fraying with each passing moment. The air grew heavy with anticipation, and an icy dread coiled in the pit of his stomach.

As the ghostly figure turned, displaying nothing in its eye sockets but darkness, Foster's finger tightened on the trigger, his aim unwavering. He was met with a sight that sent shockwaves of terror through his veins.

The ghostly presence, with an unnatural slowness, extended his right hand to the folds of his jacket, fingers curling around an unseen object hidden within. Foster's heart pounded in his chest as the figure, with agonizing deliberation, withdrew its hand to reveal a grotesque and chilling truth—a suicide vest.

Without hesitation, Foster unleashed a barrage of shotgun blasts which echoed through the room like thunder. Shell casings danced on the floor. The figure, or whatever remained of it, was torn apart by the torrent of pellets, the once-threatening object now reduced to tatters. It toppled over onto the floor, leaving a haunting hiss of the terror it had instilled.

Breathing heavily, Foster approached the fallen object cautiously, his senses on high alert. His trembling hands worked to replace shotgun with new shells. As he drew closer, a chilling realization washed over him. The object was not a person but a mannequin, a sinister ruse designed to invoke fear and chaos.

With further examination, on the floor to the side of the mannequin, Foster discovered an electric cord snaking its way from under the organ to a small generator concealed by a pile of rubbage. The truth began to unravel before him—the room had been rigged with a nightmarish charade, a malevolent performance designed to toy with his sanity.

The sinister forces at work in the house were more cunning and elaborate than he could have ever imagined, and Foster knew that he was in a deadly game with an opponent whose motives remained shrouded in darkness.

Foster's laughter, though laced with sarcasm, was a release of tension that had coiled tightly within him. The bizarre theatricality of the situation couldn't be denied, and he found a grim amusement in the elaborate hoax that had unfolded.

"Good job, Arab," he remarked wryly, his gaze sweeping across the room as if appreciating the effort that had gone into crafting this eerie spectacle. "I have to admit, you got me on this one. What's next, coward? Maybe giant spiders, or how about snakes invading the house."

The room bore the scars of the surreal performance, a testament to the lengths his unseen adversary had gone to unnerve him. Foster's analytical mind couldn't help but consider the resources expended to orchestrate such an elaborate charade. "This whole gig must have cost you a lot," he mused aloud, his voice carrying a mix of begrudging respect and curiosity.

With the air of a seasoned soldier, Foster continued, his tone resolute, "Just make sure my $25,000 is ready." The promise of the monetary prize persevered, a beacon of motivation that drove him forward despite the supernatural horrors that surrounded him. "I can sense the first light of dawn approaching," he added, his words carrying an air of finality.

As the room's eerie ambiance persisted, Foster knew that the night was far from over. The Arab's enigmatic challenges had pushed him to the brink, but he was determined to confront the mysteries of the house head-on. With the promise of sunrise on the horizon, the final chapter of this chilling tale was about to unfold, and Foster prepared to face whatever awaited him in the mansion's shadowy depths.

Now, aware of the limited time before the sun would truly rise, Foster retraced his steps through the expansive house, the flashlight casting eerie shadows that seemed to dance to the unsettling rhythm of his thoughts. The encounter with the apparition had left him both intrigued and unnerved, a tantalizing hint of the mansion's secrets and the Arab's cryptic agenda.

Returning to the kitchen, he carefully switched off his flashlight, allowing the soft glow of the candle to illuminate the room. The feeble candlelight played tricks on the walls, casting flickering specters that seemed to mimic the very apparitions he had encountered earlier. Foster couldn't help but long for a simple ice pack to soothe his throbbing head, the relentless ordeal taking its toll on his endurance.

"Focus, Foster, focus," he muttered to himself as he scoured the room for more aspirin, his head throbbing from the series of eerie events that had unfolded in the haunted house and the fall. He desperately needed to make sense of it all and devise a strategy to confront whatever supernatural forces might lay ahead.

His mind began to dissect the occurrences in the house, each one more unsettling than the last. First, there was the unsettling laughter, the eerie groans, and the blood-curdling female screams that had sporadically pierced the silence. Foster contemplated the possibility that these sounds could be easily replicated using hidden microphones strategically placed to activate with his every move. It was a clever, albeit unsettling, tactic.

Then, there was the mysterious, paralyzing gaze that had caused him to stumble and fall. Could it be that Hassan had tampered with the staircase, weakening it just enough to give way when Foster descended the steps? The thought was demonic, but it was certainly a plausible explanation.

Next on the list was the haunting image of the mannequin playing the organ. Foster couldn't help but acknowledge that it had been deliberately placed there, its mechanical movements fueled by a hidden generator. The illusion was designed to send a chill down his spine, and it had succeeded.

But what about that ghostly presence that had seemed to float at the top of the main staircase? Foster scratched his head, baffled by the illusion. Perhaps it was achieved through the use of animatronics, similar to those found in amusement rides at Disneyland.

It made sense—the figure had an otherworldly quality, and animatronics could replicate such eerie movements with precision.

Memories flooded back to Foster, reminiscent of his childhood visits to the Haunted Mansion at Disneyland, an eerie attraction where spectral figures and ghouls seemed to come alive. He could vividly recall those spine-tingling moments when ghostly apparitions occupied the seat next to him, or when they danced a macabre waltz in the grand ballroom.

In those days, he had marveled at the seamless blend of technology and artistry that brought the supernatural to life. It was all a carefully orchestrated illusion, just like what he was experiencing now in this haunted house. Foster couldn't help but draw a parallel between his current predicament and those memories from his past.

"Yes, that's it," Foster mused to himself, drawing a connection between the two. "Hassan must be employing the same principles used in those attractions at the Haunted Mansion."

He couldn't help but appreciate the ingenuity behind it all. The way animatronics, hidden mechanisms, and cleverly timed effects had been employed in the Haunted Mansion to create a truly immersive experience was a testament to the art of deception. It was clear that Hassan had taken inspiration from such attractions to craft his own haunting masterpiece.

CHAPTER ELEVEN

Foster's determination to unravel the secrets of the haunted house deepened as he thought about the intricacies of the illusions at play. He knew that uncovering the truth would require him to delve further into the mind of the mastermind behind this supernatural spectacle, all while drawing upon his own experiences with the fantastic and the uncanny.

With a sense of clarity emerging, Foster pieced together the elements of deception used by whoever was orchestrating this supernatural spectacle. Hidden microphones, tampered stairs, strategically placed mannequins, and eerie animatronics all contributed to the unsettling ambiance of the haunted house. But there was also the possibility that someone was in fact, in the house watching his every move and deciding what buttons to push.

As he contemplated these possibilities, Foster's determination to uncover the truth grew stronger.

He knew he had to delve deeper into the mysteries of this sinister place, uncovering the secrets behind the illusions, and ultimately confronting the mind behind this terrifying charade.

Taking a few more headache tablets, he grimaced at the sharp pain that pulsed through his temples. With a deep sigh, he finished off the remaining coffee in his thermos, the bitter warmth offering a meager respite from the chilling atmosphere that clung to the room.

Exhausted and weary, Foster decided to give in to his fatigue, lowering his head to rest upon the table's cold surface. With his Sig Sauer in hand, he closed his eyes, the house seemed to hold its breath, the quietude that had settled over the kitchen contrasting sharply with the night's prior chaos. The minutes ticked away slowly, each second an agonizing reminder of the impending dawn.

And then, just as he began to drift into a restless slumber, the house came alive once more. The ghastly laughter, louder and more menacing than before, echoed through the walls, resonating in Foster's ears like a haunting refrain. It was a sound that seemed to defy the boundaries of reality, a sinister presence that refused to be silenced.

But it was not alone. A woman's voice, filled with terror and urgency, pierced the chilling night air with a cry in Arabic. Foster's eyes snapped open, his heart pounding in his chest as he realized that the mansion's evil had not yet run its course. The nightmare continued, and Foster knew that the horrors of this cursed place were far from over.

A door appeared that slowly opened on its own. Foster pointed his Sig Sauer and the darkness beyond and listened for any movement. Hearing none, he cautiously approached, flashing in hand.

Foster began to enter the room, his heart pounding, his vision blurred by the tears that had welled up in his eyes that had formed while he was asleep. He leaned against the wall, his breath ragged, and wiped the sweat from his brow. The images from that room still clung to him, refusing to let go.

As he stood there, trying to regain his composure, he became aware of a soft, haunting melody that came from the interior of the room. The sound seemed to seep through the cracks in the walls, wrapping around him like a melancholic embrace. It was a melody he knew all too well—the mournful notes of a harmonica playing in the Afghan desert, a tune that had accompanied him on countless lonely nights.

With trembling hands, Foster followed the sound in the room. There he witnessed a scene straight out of his past—a moonlit night in the heart of the warzone.

In the dimly lit room, he saw himself sitting by a campfire, the embers casting flickering shadows on his face. Beside him sat his fellow SEALs, their faces etched with exhaustion and determination. In the center of their makeshift camp, a comrade played a haunting tune on his harmonica, the music drifting on the night air like a fragile promise of hope. He lowered his sidearm.

Foster watched, unable to tear his gaze away, as the memory played out before him. The camaraderie, the laughter, the shared stories of home—all of it was there, frozen in time. He could almost feel the warmth of the fire, taste the gritty sand in his mouth, and hear the distant echoes of gunfire.

But he knew that this memory was a double-edged sword. It was a reminder of the bond he had shared with his brothers, but it was also a painful testament to what he had lost. The faces around the fire began to blur, their voices fading into the distance, replaced by a deafening silence.

The room itself seemed to come alive, the walls transforming into the unforgiving desert sands that had witnessed their battles. The flames of the campfire grew higher, casting long, dancing shadows that played tricks on Foster's weary mind. He could feel the suffocating weight of his gear, the relentless heat of the Afghan sun beating down on him.

In that moment, Foster realized that he was no longer an observer of the past; he was reliving it, trapped in a nightmarish loop of time and memory. Panic surged through him as he fought to break free from the room's grasp.

He stumbled backward, his boots scraping against the rough floor. The harmonica's mournful tune grew louder, more haunting, echoing in his ears like a dirge for the fallen. Foster's breath came in ragged gasps as he forced himself to turn away, to flee from the relentless grip of the room.

As he stumbled back into the corridor, the door slammed shut behind him, the haunting melody abruptly silenced. Foster leaned against the closed door, his chest heaving, his mind reeling. The flames, the harmonica, the memories—they all clung to him like a suffocating shroud.

Haunted by the past, Foster knew he had to press on, to confront whatever other horrors awaited him in the depths of the haunted house. But the scars of that room, the guilt and pain of those lost in the flames, would stay with him, a reminder of the heavy burden he carried from his time in the field.

Feeling he had returned to the safety of the kitchen, his vision became blurry, and his eyes filled with more tears. He found himself entering another room bathed in an eerie blue light, casting long, ghostly shadows on the cracked wallpaper. Foster's heart raced as he recognized the scene before him—a dimly lit cave, damp with the sweat and fear of his past. He could hear the whispers of his fellow SEALs, their hushed voices echoing in his mind.

"Move in quietly, boys. We've got a high-value target in here," Foster whispered, his hand on the shoulder of the man in front of him.

The room seemed to come alive, the cave's walls pulsating and oozing with memories of a mission gone awry. He could hear the muffled cries of the villagers they'd hoped to protect, see the desperation in their eyes as they begged for their lives.

Foster stumbled backward, his heart pounding, the haunted room fading into the present. He shook his head, trying to dispel the memories that threatened to consume him.

The next room was even more unsettling. As he stepped inside, the air grew thick with the acrid smell of burning wreckage. Foster found himself transported to a nightmarish scene from his past—a convoy of military vehicles engulfed in flames, the searing heat and blinding smoke choking the life out of his comrades.

He saw himself, a younger, more naive version of Falcon, desperately trying to save his brothers in arms. But the fire was relentless, devouring everything in its path. Foster's hands trembled as he relived the helplessness he felt that day, the guilt of not being able to save them all.

The room seemed to feed off his torment, the flames dancing around him, mocking him with their relentless hunger. Foster stumbled out of the room, gasping for air, his body drenched in sweat.

As he moved deeper into the haunted house, he encountered more rooms that echoed his past traumas. A room filled with the deafening roar of gunfire, a room with the suffocating sandstorm of the Afghan desert, and a room with the haunting cries of children caught in the crossfire.

Each room was a relentless assault on his senses, a cruel reminder of the scars that he carried from his time in the field. Foster realized that the real ghosts he faced weren't supernatural; they were the demons of his own making.

As he continued his harrowing journey through the mansion, Foster began to question his own bravery. Was he truly fearless, or was he simply running from the ghosts of his past? The answers were elusive, hidden in the shadows of his own psyche.

And so, he pressed on, confronting the haunting memories that had defined his life as a Navy SEAL. Little did he know that the final room held the most sinister revelation of all, one that would force him to confront the darkest corners of his soul and question the very essence of his identity.

CHAPTER TWELVE

As Foster pondered the elaborate schemes that Hassan had set in motion within the mansion, a chilling comparison struck him like a bolt of lightning. It was as if the Arab had taken a page from the playbook of the Viet Cong who had once expertly rigged the maze of tunnels of Chu Chi in Vietnam. This realization sent a shiver down Foster's neck raising the hairs on his arms, driving home the extent of his adversary's cunning and the treacherous nature of the task ahead.

With the precision and caution of a seasoned soldier, Foster recognized the need to approach each new development methodically, as if planning a critical mission in the heat of battle. He knew that impulsive actions could prove fatal in this nightmarish game, and so he whispered to himself like a mantra, "Think, Foster. Plan before executing your next move."

His mind became a battlefield of strategy and anticipation, a mental chessboard where each step carried the weight of life and death. He knew that the answers lay hidden within the mansion's dark recesses, but he couldn't afford to stumble blindly into the unknown. The house was a formidable adversary, and Foster was determined to match its cunning with his own brand of calculated resolve.

The sudden presence of a cool breeze from the second floor struck Foster as odd, especially considering that he hadn't noticed it during his previous visit. It was as if an unseen current was flowing down the staircase, leading him toward the uppermost level of the mansion. He couldn't dismiss this phenomenon as a mere coincidence; the house seemed to possess a rhythm and purpose all its own.

With the instincts of a seasoned Navy SEAL, Foster's mind whirred with memories of his time in Afghanistan. He recalled the countless missions where he had climbed to higher ground to establish overwatch positions. In those desolate and unforgiving landscapes, the elevated vantage points had often been the key to successful reconnaissance. His military training echoed in his thoughts as he considered the significance of this newfound breeze.

"Think, Foster," he murmured to himself, his voice a quiet reassurance in the eerie silence of the mansion. "Think of how many times in Afghanistan you had to climb to become overwatch. The highest ground gave the best reconnaissance, remember?"

As he ascended the stairs, he couldn't help but draw a parallel between his military experience and the enigmatic challenges presented by the house. The breeze, like a beckoning call, urged him onward, and Foster steeled himself for the unsettling revelations that awaited him on the uppermost level of the mansion. It was a journey into the unknown, where his training and instincts would be put to the ultimate test.

The breeze that had accompanied Foster on his ascent ceased as he finally reached one of the mansion's bell towers. It was a location that must have, at one point in the mansion's storied past, offered a commanding view of the surrounding landscape. From this vantage point, one could have surveilled the area with a 360-degree perspective, and the strategic possibilities were evident.

As Foster's thoughts meandered through the memories of his military service, the once-familiar landscape below took on a surreal and unsettling transformation. Peering down from the bell tower, he could discern a group of SEALs, much like himself, advancing methodically down a side street in Kamesh. They moved with practiced precision, going door to door along a dusty street, an unmistakable echo of missions from his past.

In a disconcerting twist, Foster realized that his clothing had transformed to match the attire he had worn on countless missions. His baseball hat sat firmly on his head, worn backward to ensure it wouldn't obstruct his view as he prepared to take those critical sniper shots. An earpiece was securely in place, relaying updates on the advancing SEAL team's progress as they awaited his response, the weight of their trust and reliance on his reconnaissance heavy on his shoulders.

The mansion seemed to have transcended the boundaries of reality, merging Foster's past experiences with his present challenges in an uncanny and perplexing fusion. He couldn't shake the feeling that he was being drawn into a surreal reenactment of his military career, and the eerie familiarity of it all filled him with a creeping sense of dread. The bell tower had become both a vantage point and a portal to a nightmarish past, and Foster could only wonder what lay ahead in this perplexing and sinister game.

To his left, in this surreal amalgamation of reality and memory, Foster's gaze fell upon a young Afghan girl, her age not more than ten, emerging from a modest apartment. She began to walk purposefully toward the SEAL team, her diminutive figure an incongruous presence amidst the eerie tableau. Instinctively, Foster reached for his microphone, his voice a steady and authoritative command that resonated with the team below. "Hold your position," he instructed them, and the SEALs, disciplined and obedient, complied without question.

As he watched the young girl, a sense of disquiet settled over Foster. The door of the apartment swung open once more, revealing an older woman, likely the girl's mother, frantically calling out to her child. Her cries pierced the air, but the young girl remained undeterred, her path unyielding as she continued her march toward the SEALs. Foster's pulse quickened, and his trigger finger tensed involuntarily. "Hold your position. I have a young girl and older woman at 12 o'clock. The girl and woman are walking right towards your position."

Beads of sweat cascaded down his furrowed brow, falling like a waterfall onto the sandbag that supported his sniper rifle. His heart pounded in his chest, and his breaths grew shallow as he bore witness to the heart-wrenching scene playing out before him.

The young girl, oblivious to her mother's pleas, raised her right arm, revealing a chilling activation device. It was then, in the tensest of moments, that Foster's finger squeezed the trigger, the familiar recoil of his rifle punctuating the air.

In the fraction of a second that followed, reality warped and twisted around him once more. The haunting vision of the Afghan girl and her deadly payload dissolved, leaving Foster disoriented and bewildered. As if abruptly yanked from a nightmare, he found himself back in the dimly lit kitchen, his head resting upon his folded arms.

The experience left him with a profound sense of unease and the lingering question of whether the mansion was showing him more than mere illusions. Foster couldn't shake the feeling that he was being subjected to a surreal test, one that probed the depths of his past experiences and fears. With each passing moment, the line between reality and nightmare blurred further, and he braced himself for the chilling uncertainties that lay ahead in this perplexing and sinister game. He instinctively glanced at his watch, then remembered it was damaged in the fall.

It was only after Foster's disorienting journey between the haunting apparitions and the chilling memories that he became aware of a disconcerting detail. He observed, with a mixture of puzzlement and dread, that droplets of blood adorned one of his sleeves. A slow realization dawned on him as he gingerly touched his nose, finding it wet and sticky. He was bleeding, a crimson trickle seeping from his left nostril.

For a seasoned Navy SEAL accustomed to enduring extreme conditions and intense situations, this was an unusual occurrence. Foster's initial reaction was one of mild surprise, a flicker of concern briefly crossing his features. He swiftly brought his sleeve to his nose, staunching the flow of blood, and with a casual resolve, he wiped the evidence away.

As he did so, Foster couldn't help but think of the practicalities. In his line of work, a damaged shirt was a minor inconvenience. He smirked, the thought of an extra $25,000 serving as a fitting incentive to purchase a new one. It was a testament to his unflinching determination and ability to maintain composure even in the face of the supernatural horrors that surrounded him.

With the knowledge that his physical well-being remained intact, at least for the time being, Foster continued to navigate the enigmatic mansion. The mysteries that lay ahead were inscrutable, and he was resolved to unravel them, no matter the cost to his shirt or his sanity. Still, the thought that he may have a brain injury from the fall was in the back of his mind.

CHAPTER THIRTEEN

The grotesque laughter resounded through the house once more, its sinister echoes reverberating in Foster's ears like a nightmarish refrain. Despite the unsettling nature of the situation, he couldn't help but summon a measure of bravery in the face of the unknown.

"What's this, Hassan?" Foster's voice cut through the eerie laughter, his tone laced with a wry mixture of frustration and amusement. "Round two, or three, or four? I lost count." His words dripped with sarcasm, a defense mechanism honed through years of facing danger head-on. "You better have your A-game devices ready. I'd really like to see some of those animatronic devices if you have some more. What no skeletons or black cats? Guess you Arabs don't really know how to create a haunted house."

The house had become a twisted arena, a stage where reality and illusion danced in macabre harmony.

Foster's indomitable spirit, though tested, remained unbroken. "I can already feel the sun on my face," he declared with a hint of defiance, determined to press forward in this surreal contest of wits and wills. The Arab's enigmatic challenges had pushed him to the brink, but Foster's resolve burned brighter than ever as he confronted the horrors of the mansion.

Foster's heart skipped a beat as an abrupt and discordant noise shattered the eerie silence of the first floor. Every fiber of his being went on high alert, and with his Sig Sauer pistol held firmly in his hand, he moved stealthily towards the origin of the unsettling sound. In this enigmatic mansion, where every corner seemed to harbor a secret, caution had become his most trusted companion.

Using his flashlight, he followed a dimly lit hallway that branched off from the kitchen, Foster's steps were measured and deliberate. He had learned not to underestimate the evil forces at play within these walls. The mansion was like a labyrinth of mysteries, and he was determined to navigate its treacherous corridors with utmost care. The storm outside seemed to worsen as if telling him that a climax was about to happen.

His fingers tightened around the cold, reassuring grip of his firearm, the weight of it grounding him in reality amidst the surreal and unsettling atmosphere. Foster knew that he needed to confront whatever lay behind that door; there was no turning back now.

Upon reaching the door, he hesitated for a moment, his gaze fixed on the aged wood and ornate carvings that adorned its surface. It was as if the door had materialized out of thin air, a perplexing addition to an already perplexing environment. Foster couldn't shake the feeling that something significant lay beyond it, something that demanded his attention.

"I swear, that door wasn't there earlier," he muttered to no one in particular, voicing the disconcerting thought that had taken hold of his mind. It was as if the house itself was a living entity, reshaping its corridors and secrets in response to his presence. "I'm positive. This damn door was not here."

With a deep breath and resolve burning in his eyes, Foster slowly reached out for the doorknob, ready to confront whatever lay on the other side.

As he touched the door it opened and slammed shut before Foster could react. His finger hovered over the trigger, ready to unleash another barrage of bullets as soon as he revealed the threat. With a swift, calculated movement, he kicked the door open, only to be met with a bewildering sight.

Before him stood an impenetrable stone wall, as solid as any he had ever encountered. It was a confounding and disorienting moment, and Foster couldn't help but pound his fist against the unyielding surface, hoping for some sign of weakness or escape.

The mansion's ghostly architecture seemed to revel in its ability to confound and confine him, leaving

Foster to grapple with the unsettling notion that the rules of reality had been rewritten within its walls.

Driven by a growing urgency to escape the many booby traps of the house, Foster hurried to the nearest window, his heart pounding with a mix of frustration and dread. The once-grand curtains, now tattered and decayed, provided no respite as he tore them down, revealing yet another disheartening discovery.

The window, much like the door he had encountered earlier, had been sealed off with bricks, as if mocking his attempts to break free. It was as though the very fabric of the mansion resisted his every move, conspiring to keep him within its shadowy clutches. He found a heavy chair and threw it at the bricks only to shatter the piece of furniture.

Foster's frustration simmered beneath the surface as he grappled with the surreal and oppressive reality of his situation. The mansion's relentless torment showed no sign of abating, and he was left with the chilling realization that escape might prove more elusive than he had ever imagined. This was no longer just a game. It was a fight for his life.

Foster's frustration and anger grew with each discovery of the house's insidious traps. The walls closing in on him, the bricked-up windows, and the confounding dead ends had pushed him to his limits. As he stood there, facing another sealed-off window, he couldn't help but unleash his mounting frustration. And now, to add more torment, the laughter returned.

"Okay, Arab," Foster muttered through clenched teeth, his voice carrying an edge of defiance. "Is that the plan? You seal me up inside this house, thinking you can save your precious $25,000?" He paused, his words laden with a simmering anger. "Don't forget, I have witnesses back in your bar. They heard your dare, and they'll tell the police about it. They'll force you to reveal this location."

His tone was accusatory, aimed squarely at the unseen adversary who had ensnared him in this torturous game. Foster's bravado, while tested, remained intact, and he had no intention of giving in to the Arab's torment without a fight. "You didn't think of that, did you, you coward?" He spat the words with a biting sarcasm, determined to expose the Arab's recklessness in the face of his own resilience.

Another door further down the hallway began creaking open with an eerie invitation, beckoning to Foster from the depths of the mansion's shadows. Despite the relentless trials he had endured, Foster's resolve remained unshaken, his determination to confront whatever lay ahead undiminished. Sunrise should be any minute. He could feel it.

"Still want to play coward?" Foster muttered, his voice edged with a blend of defiance and dark humor. He had faced countless dangers in his life, both on the battlefield and beyond, and this eerie mansion was just another adversary to be conquered. "What the hell, I'm game."

With that, he lowered his shotgun from his shoulder, the cold steel resting in his grasp like an extension of his willpower. Each step forward was a testament to his indomitable spirit, a fearless soldier's resolve that had carried him through the darkest of days. Foster was prepared to venture into the unknown once more, determined to uncover the secrets and face the horrors that awaited him beyond the slowly opening door.

This room was unlike any other Foster had explored so far. It was a large chamber filled with an array of mirrors, each one reflecting a different version of himself. He couldn't help but raise an eyebrow at the peculiar sight. "What's this? Your own little funhouse?" Foster muttered to himself, his voice tinged with a hint of skepticism.

The feeble light from his flickering flashlight danced erratically across the myriad mirrors, casting fragmented images of himself all around the room. He took cautious steps further into the room, the uneven reflections playing tricks on his perception. The mirrors seemed to stretch endlessly in every direction, creating a bewildering maze of distorted reflections.

As Foster moved deeper into the room, the atmosphere grew increasingly unsettling. The air felt heavy, as if it held secrets long buried within these glassy surfaces. He couldn't help but feel a sense of foreboding, as if the very walls were closing in on him.

Foster's reflection, fractured into countless pieces, stared back at him from all directions. He watched as his own face contorted with confusion, mirroring his internal struggle to make sense of this bizarre room. The room seemed to mock him, as if it knew his weaknesses and fears.

A sudden realization struck him like a bolt of lightning. The mirrors weren't just reflecting his current self; they were showing him fragments of his past. The images shifted, and Foster found himself transported back to some of the most harrowing moments from his time as a Navy SEAL.

In one mirror, he saw himself trapped underwater, struggling against the currents as he rescued a fellow comrade during a covert mission. The memory was vivid, and Foster could feel the pressure of the water crushing him, the panic of running out of breath. He tried to tear his gaze away, but the reflection held him captive.

In another mirror, he witnessed a tense hostage rescue operation, his heart pounding as he navigated a labyrinthine maze of narrow corridors. The reflection showed the fear and determination etched across his face as he fought to save innocent lives. The memories played out before him, as if he were reliving those missions all over again.

Foster's breath quickened, and beads of sweat formed on his forehead. The room had become a chamber of horrors, a place where his past demons came back to haunt him. He stumbled back, trying to escape the relentless images, but the mirrors seemed to follow him, each one revealing a different chapter of his military career.

Another mirror had an Afghani male being held down underwater while interrogators through questions and insults at him. Foster turned away from the mirror only to see an American soldier being beheaded in a street whose name he had long forgotten.

As the reenactments of his heroic assignments continued to play out in the mirrors, Foster couldn't help but wonder if Hassan had somehow tapped into his deepest fears and regrets. He needed to find a way out of this room and regain control of the situation, but the mirrors held him in their thrall, their relentless reflections refusing to release him from their grip.

He tried to remember the route back to the door he had entered. He felt he had made progress when he came face to face with the largest mirror in the room. It called to him. He focused as best he could, noticing that his nose had started to bleed again as well as a few drops from both of his ears.

The mirror at first seemed to show smoke or mist coming from the ground. Then, mixed in with the mist, various images appeared of his kills. Grossly disfigured and in various stages of decay, they rose from the base of the mirror and after coming towards him, rose up to the top before disappearing, only for the next specter to appear.

Foster couldn't bear to look at the mirror any longer. The grotesque images of his past deeds and the spectral apparitions had pushed him to the brink of terror. He pivoted on his heels, desperately attempting to escape the horrifying reflections, but it seemed the mirror was determined to torment him.

As his gaze veered away from the mirror, the haunting laughter that had intermittently echoed through the house grew louder and more sinister. It reverberated through the room, a chilling symphony of torment that clawed at his sanity. His shotgun slipped from his trembling fingers, clattering to the ground as he grappled with the overwhelming dread coursing through him.

Foster's heart pounded in his chest as he clamped his hands over his ears in a futile attempt to drown out the haunting laughter. The very walls of the room seemed to close in, suffocating him with their evil intent. The relentless laughter pierced his soul, driving him to the edge of madness.

Seconds felt like hours as Foster endured the nightmarish auditory onslaught. The laughter seemed to seep into his very being, each sinister chuckle latching onto his psyche like a parasite. He could feel his grip on reality slipping, his thoughts spiraling into a terrifying abyss.

Then, just as suddenly as it had begun, the laughter ceased. The room fell into an eerie silence, broken only by Foster's ragged breaths. He cautiously lowered his trembling hands from his ears, his heart still pounding in his chest. As he surveyed the room, he noticed that the mirror, once a grotesque display of his haunting past, had returned to a clear, pristine surface.

Foster's relief was short-lived. As he examined his trembling hands, he saw that they were covered in blood. Panic surged through him as he realized that the blood wasn't his own; it had materialized on his palms as if it had seeped from the very walls of this accursed room.

The implications of this supernatural ordeal weighed heavily on Foster's mind. It was as though the mirror had not only dredged up his past sins but had also drawn blood as a sinister tribute to his torment. He wiped his hands on his clothes, but the unsettling sensation lingered, as if the room itself had borne witness to his suffering.

Foster knew he had to escape this room, this house, before it consumed him entirely. With his shotgun back in hand, he took a deep breath and steeled himself for whatever terrors lay ahead. The challenge Hassan had presented was far more deadly than he could have ever imagined, and Foster was determined to uncover its secrets and confront the darkness that had taken hold of this haunted house.

CHAPTER FOURTEEN

Foster steadied his nerves as he stepped away from the terrifying mirror room. His mind raced, calculating the time until sunrise. With each passing moment, the weight of the challenge he had accepted grew heavier, and he knew that the house's supernatural horrors were far from over.

Continuing his treacherous journey down the seemingly endless hallway, Foster was acutely aware of the mounting tension in the air. He had left behind the room filled with tormenting reflections, but he couldn't shake the feeling that the house itself was a living, malevolent entity. Every creak of the floorboards and every flicker of the dim lights seemed like a sinister omen.

As he pressed on, he heard the door to the mirror room slam shut behind him, the echoing sound startling him. He refused to let fear paralyze him; he had to confront Hassan and expose the truth behind these elaborate tricks.

With determination, he called out into the darkened corridor, his voice echoing through the haunted house. “Sorry, Arab,” he taunted, his tone laced with defiance. “Your tricks are becoming predictable. Have you checked your watch? Sunrise is almost here.”

The silence that followed was deafening, broken only by the soft patter of his own footsteps. Foster’s senses were on high alert, and he strained to hear any response from Hassan. But the house remained eerily quiet, as if it were holding its breath, waiting for the final act of their sinister game.

As he ventured deeper into the darkness, Foster couldn’t help but wonder if he had underestimated the true nature of the dare. It was becoming clear that there was more to this house than mere illusions and tricks. The supernatural forces at play were beyond anything he had encountered in his military career.

With the minutes ticking away and the first hints of dawn’s light beginning to pierce the darkness outside, Foster knew that Hassan was running out of time. For Foster, the challenge had become a battle for his very survival, and he was determined to emerge victorious, no matter the cost.

“Got something new, Hassan? The sun is almost up and you lose,” Foster jokingly said, his voice tinged with a mixture of courage and unease. He couldn’t deny the growing sense of fear that had settled upon him like a heavy shroud. The sinister tricks and tormenting illusions had become tiresome, and Foster was ready to confront the man behind them.

As if in response to his challenge, the hallway around him seemed to come alive with a disconcerting presence. Soft, almost imperceptible whispers began to emanate from the very walls, their insidious voices carrying an eerie, disembodied quality. Foster strained to hear, his instincts alert to the ever-increasing murmurs.

The whispers swelled in volume, a choir of voices that seemed to seep from the very cracks and crevices of the house. Foster's heart quickened as he realized that the voices were speaking in Arabic, their words a haunting echo of his past. Questions arose in the unfamiliar language, their accusatory tone chilling him to the bone.

"Why did you kill us?" the voices murmured, their words laden with sorrow and anger. The accusations hung in the air like a palpable presence, each syllable driving deeper into Foster's conscience. The tormenting echoes seemed to reverberate within his very soul.

Foster's breaths came in ragged gasps as he struggled to make sense of the relentless accusations. Faces from his past assignments, those he had been forced to eliminate in the line of duty, seemed to materialize in the shadows. Their mournful gazes bore into him, their eyes filled with the weight of unspoken anguish.

The whispers grew louder, each voice overlapping with the next, creating a disorienting cacophony that threatened to overwhelm him. Foster's resolve wavered, and he felt a rising sense of guilt and remorse gnawing at his conscience. The accusations were tearing him apart, forcing him to confront the moral complexity of his actions.

Desperation clawed at him as he continued down the ever-darkening hallway, his steps faltering but determined. He had to find Hassan, confront him, and end this torment once and for all. The walls seemed to close in around him, the relentless whispers threatening to consume him entirely.

Foster's mind raced, searching for a way to silence the haunting voices and escape this nightmarish ordeal. The challenge had evolved into something far more sinister than he could have ever imagined, and the house itself had become a hellish entity, intent on unraveling the very fabric of his soul.

Foster's nerves were frayed, and the relentless whispers of accusation echoing through the haunted house had pushed him to his breaking point. Desperation clawed at his chest as he raised his shotgun, the weight of the weapon offering some semblance of comfort in this nightmarish place. He had to take action; he had to break the cycle of torment.

With a trembling hand, he aimed the shotgun and squeezed the trigger. The deafening blast reverberated through the haunted structure, the explosion of sound shattering the eerie silence that had settled like a suffocating shroud. The walls seemed to quiver in response, and for a moment, Foster was blinded by the brilliant flash of the muzzle.

The gunshot echoed and reverberated through the house, its sheer intensity deafening to Foster, who felt a sharp pain in his ears. The sound of the shot seemed to pierce through the very fabric of the supernatural torment that had enveloped him, like a beacon of defiance in the darkness.

The impact of the gunshot had the desired effect. The ghostly whispers that had plagued him, their haunting accusations growing louder with each step, ceased abruptly. The silence that followed was eerie, as if the house itself held its breath in response to the sudden eruption of violence.

Foster's chest heaved with exertion as he lowered the shotgun, his ears ringing from the cacophonous blast. The relief he felt was palpable, as if a weight had been lifted from his shoulders. The accusing voices, the relentless torment, had finally been silenced.

But as the echoes of the gunshot faded, Foster couldn't escape the sinking feeling that he had just unleashed something far more sinister. The ghostly forces that dwelled within the house were unpredictable, and he had no way of knowing the consequences of his actions.

With his shotgun still in hand, Foster braced himself for whatever might come next. The challenge

Hassan had presented had taken a dark and twisted turn, and Foster was prepared to confront the horrors that awaited him. The haunted structure seemed to hold its breath, as if the very walls were waiting for the next move in this deadly game of wits and courage.

CHAPTER FIFTEEN

Foster had reached his limit. The relentless horrors and supernatural ordeals he'd faced in the haunted house had tested his mettle beyond imagination. He couldn't help but marvel at the macabre creativity behind Hassan's twisted challenges, but he had his limits. With a voice trembling from a mixture of fear and frustration, he addressed the unseen orchestrator of this nightmarish spectacle.

"You know, Hassan," Foster began, his tone laced with a heavy dose of fatigue and defiance, "I've been at death's door more times than I can count. Your little Halloween pranks, though magically entertaining, are no substitute for the real-life experiences this old Navy SEAL has encountered." He paused, taking a moment to collect himself as he scanned the shadowy surroundings.

The haunted house seemed to listen, the eerie stillness punctuated only by the faintest creaks and whispers. Foster squared his shoulders and continued, his voice carrying through the oppressive silence. "You can call the game right now. Pay me my money, and I promise I won't rub it in back at your bar. What do you say, Arab?"

The echoes of his words hung in the air, the weight of the challenge was heavy. Foster's proposition was both a plea for mercy and a test of Hassan's resolve. He couldn't help but wonder if the man behind these horrors would finally reveal himself or if the game would persist, dragging him deeper into the abyss of the unknown.

As Foster stood there, shotgun in hand, he couldn't escape the feeling that he was being watched, scrutinized from the shadows. The moments ticked by, the oppressive silence pressing down on him like an invisible force. In the eerie stillness, he found himself holding his breath, waiting for a response that could mean the difference between escape and eternal torment.

"Alright, fine. We'll play it your way," Foster grumbled with a begrudging acceptance of the ongoing torment. He couldn't deny the audacious creativity behind Hassan's sinister game, but the exhaustion had taken its toll.

"But I want you to know, Arab, I'm exhausted," he continued, his voice carrying the weight of his physical and emotional fatigue. "I hope you've got some other tricks up your sleeve, because right now,

I'm headed for the kitchen. I need to take a seat and swallow a few headache pills."

Foster paused, letting the words hang in the air for a moment, then added with a wry smile, "Do you hear what I hear? Tick, tick, tick. Start getting that money ready. The game is almost over coward. I win." His tone was a mixture of bravado and weariness, a testament to his determination to see this challenge through to the end.

In the kitchen, Foster noticed a stark contrast to the rest of the house. Here, the once-deafening horrors that had plagued him had fallen silent. The hideous laughter and screaming that had echoed through the haunted house had disappeared, leaving behind only the normal sounds of an aging structure.

As he moved further into the kitchen, the house seemed to breathe around him, its timeworn structure creaking and settling. The coolness of the night was giving way to the advancing warmth of the approaching sunrise. Foster couldn't help but appreciate the newfound tranquility, even as he remained on high alert for what might come next. The absence of the supernatural torment was both a relief and a source of unease, leaving him to wonder if this respite was merely the calm before another storm.

Foster's senses heightened as he entered the kitchen, and a pungent odor began to infiltrate the air. At first, he dismissed it as the acrid smell of his sweat-soaked clothing, a consequence of his nightmarish journey through the haunted house. He hastily grabbed his military jacket, raising it to his nose to confirm his suspicions.

To his surprise, the scent was different, far more unsettling. It wasn't the stench of perspiration but something far more sinister. The aroma grew in intensity, and a grim realization dawned on him. It was the unmistakable smell of death—of bodies being stacked in a grotesque pile, reminiscent of the ancient Viking tradition of preparing for a pyre.

Foster's heart pounded as he scanned the kitchen, his trained eyes searching for the source of the macabre scent. His surroundings offered no visible clues. There was no sign of smoke or burning bodies, just the overwhelming, putrid odor that seemed to worsen with every passing moment.

Desperate to escape the noxious fumes, Foster pulled the sleeve of his jacket over his nose and mouth, hoping to filter out the nauseating stench. He couldn't comprehend how this eerie transformation had occurred so swiftly. It was as if Hassan had conjured this disturbing element to further torment him.

As he battled the overwhelming odor, Foster couldn't help but reflect on the diabolical nature of this challenge. It was clear that every room, every moment of this ordeal was meticulously crafted to test his limits and erode his resolve. The ancient Viking tradition of death and burning bodies seemed like a cruel and calculated addition by Hassan to the sinister tapestry of the haunted house.

The putrid stench that had filled the kitchen gradually dissipated, as if it were just another fearful tactic employed by Hassan. Foster's relief was tangible as he took a moment to catch his breath, realizing that he had successfully navigated yet another twisted test set before him.

Foster's temples throbbed with pain as he reached for two more headache tablets. He swallowed them with a grim determination, the bitterness of the medicine a stark reminder of the relentless trials he had endured. His body was weary, and his spirit was flagging, but he knew he couldn't succumb to exhaustion just yet.

Growing weary of the ceaseless wandering through the haunted house, Foster made a calculated decision. If Hassan had more nightmarish tricks in store for him before the sun's rays broke the horizon, he'd prefer to face them in the relative comfort of the kitchen. Weary beyond measure, he returned to the same spot where he had previously sought respite, laying his head on his folded arms in a feeble attempt to catch a few moments of rest.

With each passing minute, the anticipation weighed heavily on Foster's chest. He was trapped in a deadly game, and he had no choice but to wait for the next move, even if it meant attempting to steal a brief nap amidst the encroaching horrors. The house seemed to hold its breath, as if it, too, was waiting for the next chapter of their sinister duel to unfold.

As he drifted through the surreal landscape of his reverie, he discovered himself in the dimly lit ambiance of Hassan's bar, a grin stretching across his face, eager to regale the patrons with the tale of his recent conquest. With an air of ostentation, he proudly brandished the hefty stack of cash he had amassed from his recent endeavor.

Amidst the animated chatter and clinking glasses, Hassan, the bartender, couldn't resist revisiting the story of Foster's apparent trepidation during their expedition to the reputedly haunted house. Each time Hassan attempted to recount the spine-tingling details of Foster's supposed fear, Foster skillfully drowned out the narrative with an emphatic declaration of "BS!" His boisterous interjection was invariably accompanied by a flamboyant flourish of his newfound wealth, a display meant to underscore his audacious confidence.

The bar's patrons watched with a mixture of amusement and intrigue as Foster, immersed in his own world of bravado, continued to bask in the glory of his triumph, all the while downplaying any inkling of fear that may have tainted his supposedly fearless persona. The wad of money served as both a tangible testament to his success and a shield against the specter of fear that threatened to encroach upon his narrative, creating an atmosphere of both skepticism and admiration among those gathered around him.

Suddenly, Foster found himself in an inexplicable state, suspended in the air above a room that bore a striking resemblance to those he had encountered countless times during his tours in Afghanistan. The rough-hewn dirt floors were obscured by intricately woven rugs, and the pervasive aroma of Arab cuisine permeated the surroundings, stirring vivid memories of the past. As if beckoned by some unseen force, his ethereal form gravitated toward the faint echoes of Arabic whispers that danced through the air.

Drawn by an irresistible pull, Foster glided toward the source of these hushed conversations. From his elevated vantage point, he witnessed a scene that left him profoundly unsettled. Looking down, he beheld a young girl, her innocent countenance juxtaposed with the grim reality unfolding before his eyes. She was being assisted by an older male figure, their actions fraught with sinister purpose. Together, they were meticulously filling pockets with a chilling cargo – explosives meticulously crafted into a child-sized suicide vest.

The grotesque tableau that unfolded below Foster's spectral gaze seemed to defy reason and morality, a haunting embodiment of the horrors he had witnessed during his military service. The juxtaposition of innocence and malevolence weighed heavily on his soul as he watched this sinister preparation unfold.

The intensity of the moment reached its zenith, and Foster's heart pounded in his chest as if trying to break free from the nightmarish vision. In a frenzied jolt, he was wrenched from the dream world, his awakening accompanied by the cold sheen of sweat that clung to his trembling body. Once again, he was brought back to the harsh reality of his own existence, haunted by the disturbing images that had briefly inhabited his slumbering mind.

CHAPTER SIXTEEN

As Foster's hand instinctively reached for his thermos, he was met with a jarring realization—it was empty, devoid of the comforting warmth of the coffee that had briefly tethered him to the realm of wakefulness. The weight of exhaustion pressed upon him like an anchor, and he lowered his heavy head into his hands, finding support in the sturdy table.

Suddenly, a voice pierced the silence, interrupting his contemplative solitude. "Hello, Navy SEAL," it declared, emanating from the adjacent room. The words bore the distinct cadence of Hassan, the enigmatic figure who had become both a captor and an enigma in Foster's twisted predicament.

Foster couldn't help but think, "About time." He surmised that sunrise must have come, signaling the potential end to his ordeal within the foreboding house.

Summoning the remnants of his resolve, Foster rose from his seat and drew his Sig Sauer from its hip holster. Every step he took towards the adjacent room was fraught with caution, his senses alert for the lurking threat of booby traps that might lie in his path. To his relief, no such dangers manifested themselves along the way.

Upon entering the room, Foster's gaze was instantly drawn to a vintage black and white television screen, upon which Hassan's visage materialized, his countenance adorned with a sinister grin that sent shivers down Foster's spine.

"Have you decided to admit that you are the coward, Mr. Navy SEAL?" Hassan inquired, his tone dripping with a blend of mockery and malevolence. In response, Foster wore an equally sinister grin, tinged with sarcasm, as he selected a chair and seated himself opposite the imposing television screen.

In that charged moment, the two adversaries locked eyes, a battle of wits and willpower unfolding in the eerie confines of the house. Foster, now armed and seemingly ready to confront whatever twisted game lay ahead, was prepared to navigate the treacherous psychological terrain laid out by his captor, all while the sinister grin on Hassan's face hinted at an impending showdown of mind and mettle.

"Don't attempt to back out of our bet, Arab," Foster asserted with a steely resolve. "You've witnessed firsthand how I've deftly handled every single one of your cunning tricks you've sprung on me. I must give you credit; some of them were astonishingly lifelike. I'm still baffled by your artistry. But, as I've mentioned before, they were truly entertaining. Now, do open up this house, won't you? I'm rather eager to collect my well-earned winnings."

Hassan, wearing a sly and calculating expression, responded, "Not so hasty in claiming your victory, Mr. SEAL. How is your headache?"

Foster affected nonchalance, waving off the discomfort. "Headache? Oh, you mean that little bump on my head? I'll consult my attorney about my 'unfortunate fall.' Who knows, I might have to extract a bit more from you," he retorted with a sarcastic grin. Then, leaning in closer, he continued, "Speaking of which, I'm curious, Hassan. How many days did it take you to rig this place? Your dedication to this elaborate scheme is rather impressive."

The tension between them continued to fill the air, their exchange a verbal skirmish that hinted at deeper layers of intrigue and rivalry. Foster's determination to claim his winnings battled against Hassan's uncanny ability to weave an intricate web of challenges and uncertainties, and the question of who would emerge victorious remained shrouded in the uncertainty of the house's mysteries.

"Ah, indeed, some background information would be quite illuminating, wouldn't it?" Hassan remarked with a wry grin, acknowledging the need for context in this elaborate game of wits. "So, it took me two days to, as you put it, rig the house. Impressive work, I must admit. My technical friends were quite resourceful. And that terrorist playing the organ—quite the showpiece, I must say. Don't you agree?" Foster did not answer.

Hassan's eyes sparkled with satisfaction at Foster's acknowledgment, but his smile remained enigmatic. "I hope you enjoyed it. But," he added, his tone becoming more contemplative, "once you spotted that extension cord, I knew you were onto me. You've always had a knack for seeing through my illusions, Mr. SEAL. That's why I had to ratchet up the stakes a bit."

Foster's expression grew more serious as he recalled the moment. "Yeah, it wasn't bad at all," he conceded, "but when I saw that telltale extension cord, I had a feeling I'd unraveled part of your plan. Apologies for having to obliterate that mannequin, though. It was just my way of showing you that I had entered your house of tricks and treats fully prepared, armed to the teeth. Your little games weren't going to catch me off guard."

Their banter had an undercurrent of respect, as if both men, despite being adversaries in this bizarre contest, harbored a certain admiration for each other's cunning and resourcefulness. The atmosphere remained charged with anticipation, the next move in this high-stakes game of cat and mouse hanging in the balance.

"Alright, now that we've had our little bullshit session," Foster declared, his patience beginning to wear thin, "let's cut to the chase. Open that damn door so I can finally head home, take a shower, and then make my way to your bar to claim my winnings. Give me a couple of hours to freshen up and prepare. Two hours should suffice, I reckon."

Hassan's response was enigmatic, a subtle shift in the atmosphere indicating that this peculiar ordeal was far from over. "Oh, Falcon," he uttered, his voice laced with a newfound gravity as he used Foster's call sign for the first time. The use of that code name carried a weighty significance, hinting at deeper layers of meaning and purpose that remained hidden beneath the surface of their bizarre encounter. "The game is not over."

CHAPTER SEVENTEEN

"By the way," Foster remarked with genuine surprise, "I don't recall ever giving you my call sign, Falcon. How on earth did you come to know it?" He leaned forward, his curiosity piqued by this unexpected revelation.

Hassan's response carried an air of nonchalance, though his words hinted at a deeper understanding of Foster's past. "Oh, Falcon," he replied, his tone somewhat distant, "your fame preceded you, especially in my homeland, especially Bora Bora and Kamesh."

'The Falcon has struck' would echo through the streets after your deadly sniper attacks. How many kills did you tally before you left the service of the United States?" Hassan's casual inquiry belied the intensity of the question, as if he were probing for a hidden truth, indifferent to the weight of the answer.

"Too many to count," Falcon responded with a touch of arrogance. "You know the old saying, 'they all look the same.' After a while, my kills all just blended together." His response carried a veiled attempt to provoke a reaction from Hassan, to elicit a spark of anger or emotion. However, to his surprise, Hassan remained stoically composed, his countenance unwavering.

A pregnant pause that seemed to stretch on for an eternity. Hassan, with a wry and somewhat chilling smile gracing his lips, broke the quietude with a question that cut to the core of Foster's self-perception.

"Falcon, the man, the myth, the killer of children," Hassan began, his words delivered with a mix of irony and disdain. "This is the bravery that you hold in such high esteem. Is that what you're so proud of?"

The room seemed to close in around Foster as he grappled with Hassan's incisive inquiry. It was a moment of reckoning, an uncomfortable mirror held up to reflect the darker aspects of his past. Foster could feel the weight of his own history bearing down upon him, and he knew that this conversation had taken an unexpectedly profound turn, delving into the depths of his conscience and challenging the very foundations of his identity as Falcon.

"I served my country with honor and distinction," Foster declared with a hint of defiance in his voice. "Those I eliminated were enemies of my nation. What are you trying to prove, Hassan? Release me from this place and settle your debt, you son of a bitch." The tension in the room simmered, a volatile mixture of anger, frustration, and a gnawing need for resolution.

"Falcon," Hassan's voice grew somber, laden with a palpable weight of accusation, "do you remember a mission in Kamesh? From your sniper's nest, you coldly took the life of a young girl in the middle of the street. Can you recall the chilling scene as your comrades congratulated you on yet another kill? It was just another notch on the belt for the illustrious Falcon."

The memory Hassan had invoked hung heavily in the room, a haunting specter that seemed to cast a pall over Foster's conscience. It was a moment of profound reckoning, a stark reminder of the moral complexities that had become entwined with his past actions as a skilled marksman. The question now remained: how would Foster confront this painful chapter of his history?

Foster indeed had a clear memory of the incident. A young Afghani girl, maybe ten-years-old came out onto the street walking directly to the advancing Marines and SEALs in Kamesh. The same scene that was re-enacted in either the mirror room or during one of his restless naps. That he could not be sure, but he remembers the mission.

As the girl approached his comrades, he gave them the order to halt as he watched her through his scope. The door to the house she had come from opened and a frantic female, he presumed her mother, came running out crying and shouting for her to stop and return.

The girl would not respond, but instead, opened her light jacket and raised her right arm showing the trigger device for her suicide vest.

Hassan leaned in, his eyes fixed on Foster, his voice laced with a chilling mixture of accusation and revelation. “Ah, it’s evident from your expressions, Falcon, that you remember well. How did it feel to tighten your finger on that trigger, to witness her young chest shatter under the force of your bullet? A chest that would never develop breasts to nurture her future children.”

Foster’s throat tightened, and he attempted to regain his composure, his breaths coming in heavy and labored. Hassan’s words had struck him like a thunderbolt, unearthing memories he had long sought to bury. “Yes, Arab,” Foster admitted with a heavy heart, his voice trembling with the weight of remorse. “I remember taking her life. It was a choice between her and my team.”

Hassan nodded, his gaze unrelenting. “Just another dead camel jockey in your eyes, right, Falcon?” he continued, the bitterness in his tone unmistakable. “But that day, it wasn’t just that, was it? There’s more to that story, isn’t there?” The room seemed to close in around them, the past bearing down upon Foster with a relentless grip, forcing him to confront the full extent of his actions that fateful day in Kamesh.

“I have no idea what you’re going on about, Hassan,” Foster retorted, his frustration bubbling to the surface. "Is this just another ploy to avoid paying up? I'll tell you this, once I'm out of this place and I've collected what's owed to me, I'll make sure you regret your cowardly games. Now, quit stalling and let me out of here." The room crackled with tension, the standoff between them intensifying as the unresolved mysteries of their past loomed large.

"I'll enlighten you further, Falcon, about what transpired on that ill-fated day," Hassan continued, his voice tinged with a grim solemnity. "The woman who was chasing after the young girl arrived at the same moment as your bullet—the same bullet that passed through the fragile frame of the girl and plunged into the body of the adult. You even took pride in it, Falcon, didn't you? You quipped, 'Two birds with one shot.'"

Foster's silence was noticeable, as if he were transported back to that harrowing moment, reliving the event in his mind's eye. Finally, he responded, his voice carrying the weight of a haunting memory. "Sometimes, things unfold in unforeseen ways," he stated, his attempt at a grin faltering and fading. "It's what we call collateral damage." His words held a touch of resignation, as if he had come to accept the grim reality of the choices he had made on that fateful day in Bora Bora.

"Ah yes, 'collateral damage,' a term I became all too familiar with in Afghanistan," Hassan retorted with a hint of bitterness. "A convenient catch-all phrase to sweep your mistakes under the rug, isn't it, Falcon?" His words were charged with an accusation that cut through the room like a blade, challenging Foster to confront the moral complexities and consequences of his actions in the harsh realities of war.

"Listen, Arab," Foster responded defensively, "I'm not thrilled that two of your countrymen, or countrywomen, lost their lives. But it was a war, for God's sake. What's your point here? You came to America, probably received all sorts of handouts that ordinary Americans don't get, even started your own bar. What exactly are you complaining about?" His words were tinged with frustration and a touch of resentment, as if he couldn't comprehend why Hassan was holding him accountable for the grim realities of the battlefield.

"Yes, it seems we've arrived at the culmination of my little game, where I lay it all bare," Hassan declared, drawing nearer to the television monitor on his end.

CHAPTER EIGHTEEN

"During the war," Hassan began, his voice tinged with a mix of nostalgia and longing, "I fought alongside the Americans. I yearned for something better for my family. Kamdesh, before it fell into the clutches of ISIS, was a peaceful town. My wife and I had a child who loved going to school, and my wife was pursuing her dream of becoming a nurse."

Foster, growing impatient, interjected, "Is there a point to this conversation, Hassan? I've got matters to attend to once I'm out of this infernal house."

"Just a little more patience, Falcon," Hassan urged. "I'm almost finished. You see, when the American forces arrived to liberate our town from ISIS, I volunteered as a translator. I won't deny that my motive was to build rapport with the Americans, with the hope that after the war, my family and I could migrate to the United States. And your forces did drive ISIS out of my town."

Hassan's voice grew heavy with bitterness as he continued, "But then, your new American President, Biden, decided to start withdrawing troops from my country. Do you have any idea what that did to me and my family? While the main ISIS force retreated, many of their operatives were absorbed into neighboring factions seeking revenge on those who had aided you. That's why you found yourself in my town, Falcon, where you shot and killed my daughter and wife."

Foster's world seemed to shatter as he listened to Hassan's heart-wrenching story. He fumbled for words, his guilt weighing him down like an anchor, making it impossible to offer any adequate response. Acid built up in his stomach and throat.The realization of the consequences of his actions in a distant war zone had finally come full circle, and it was a bitter pill to swallow.

"My daughter," Hassan began, his voice quivering with the weight of unspeakable sorrow, "was compelled to don a suicide vest and make the ultimate sacrifice to protect her mother and me. The operatives of ISIS had manipulated her into believing that this was the righteous path, that through her martyrdom, her parents would be spared from the wrath of ISIS. Her love for us was so immense that she was willing to relinquish her own future." Emotion choked his words as Hassan's eyes welled with tears, his anguish visible.

Foster's mind was a turbulent sea, its waves crashing against the cliffs of his conscience as he grappled with the haunting revelations of Hassan's narrative. Staring blankly at the television screen, he seemed to have disconnected from his immediate surroundings, lost in the somber depths of his own thoughts.

The eerie stillness of the room was disrupted by a surreal and chilling moment when crimson drops of blood spattered onto his sleeves. The shock of this macabre occurrence jolted Foster out of his trance, his heart pounding as he tried to make sense of the gruesome tableau before him.

Hassan's voice, cold and unyielding, penetrated the room's oppressive silence. "Before long," he remarked with eerie calmness, "your sleeves won't suffice to stem the relentless tide of blood that will pour from your nose. I imagine you've already endured a similar fate with your ears, haven't you?"

The gravity of the situation weighed heavily on Foster, his physical and emotional suffering now tangible and undeniable. The room, once an enigmatic labyrinth of psychological torment, had transformed into a nightmarish theater where the consequences of his past actions had come to life in gruesome detail.

"You see, Falcon, after you entered the house, you placed your duffle bag on the table at the base of the stairs and went exploring. You were so brave. I took the opportunity to place a hallucinating mixture in your thermos. That is what possibly added to you fall going to the basement, but the wood in this place is almost beyond repair."

"So, you bastard, besides rigging this damn house, you doped me up trying to win at all costs. Well, Arab. You lose. Here I am, now let me out."

"Falcon, I am not through. After your fall, you eventually returned to the kitchen and tried to take a nap. Do you recall?" Not receiving an answer but seeing Foster's recollection on his face, he continued.

Hassan leaned forward, his eyes locking onto Foster's with an unsettling intensity. "When I later immigrated to the United States," he began, his voice low and conspiratorial, "I continued my work in the realm of bio-engineering, this time with your own State Department. Our endeavors were shrouded in the deepest secrecy, classified beyond measure. But since you are now in a position where you can never reveal what I am about to divulge, I shall proceed."

He paused for a moment, the gravity of his revelation settling in the room. "Our work," he continued, "centered around the realm of chemical and biological warfare, a realm so menacing that its mere existence could send shivers down the spine of any civilian population. But let me not digress further. You see, within the confines of our clandestine laboratory, we birthed a most sinister creature, a creature measuring a mere 5 to 6 centimeters in length, bearing an eerie resemblance to an earthworm."

Foster's curiosity was piqued, his senses on high alert as Hassan's narrative grew ever more enigmatic. The room seemed to crackle with a sense of foreboding, a sense that something deeply unsettling was about to be unveiled.

"Our earthworm, however," Hassan continued, his voice taking on a sinister edge, "harbors an insatiable appetite for human flesh. It's a grotesque predilection, truly disturbing. When presented with the choice between animal tissue and the delicate texture of human flesh, there's simply no comparison."

Foster's apprehension deepened as the implications of Hassan's revelation sank in. The room seemed to close in around him, and he couldn't help but feel like a pawn in a nightmarish game that had spiraled out of control. The once-secretive world of bio-engineering had unleashed an abomination, a creature with an unholy craving for human flesh, and the implications were nothing short of horrifying.

Hassan's gaze remained fixed on Foster, as if daring him to comprehend the magnitude of their shared predicament. The night had taken an even darker turn, and Foster couldn't help but wonder how he had become entangled in this surreal and sinister narrative.

"Let me out of here, Arab," Foster pleaded, his voice laced with desperation and fear. "I swear, you're a dead man," he declared, his frustration simmering with a dangerous intensity.

Hassan's response was chillingly composed, a cold smile playing on his lips. "You see, Falcon," he began, his tone carrying an eerie sense of triumph, "you've lost, after all. While you were in the kitchen, in that fitful sleep of yours, I discreetly placed one of my worms into your right ear. If you've been experiencing blood flowing from your ears, then my little worm has already begun its grim feast on the outer portion of your brain tissue."

Foster's eyes widened in horror, the reality of his predicament sinking in like an anchor to his soul. "It won't be long," Hassan continued with an unsettling calmness, "before you start to feel a tingling sensation in both your arms and blood flowing from your mouth. Fortunately for you, you shouldn't experience any pain, as my worm diligently devours you from the inside out."

Foster instantly grabbed his right arm and then his left. The room seemed to close in on Foster, the nightmare of his situation becoming all too real. He was trapped in a macabre tale of vengeance and retribution, a captive audience to his own inexorable demise.

CHAPTER NINETEEN

Blood continued to ooze from Foster's ears, staining his sleeves as he futilely wiped them clean. His voice was weak, but defiance still smoldered in his eyes. "Well played, Arab," he rasped, his words dripping with grudging admiration. "Well played. But you haven't won. No, I still hold all the cards."

With deliberate intent, Foster's trembling hand reached for his Sig Sauer pistol, the cold metal reassuring in his grip. The dimly lit room cast eerie shadows on his face as his gaze shifted from the blood-smeared table to the vintage television set, its flickering screen bathing the room in an eerie glow. A ghoulish smirk crossed his lips, and he muttered with chilling resolve, "See you in hell, Arab."

His finger tightened on the trigger, and the deafening shot pierced the air before Foster's head slammed onto the tablecloth. Blood mixed with spilled wine, creating a macabre tableau of violence and finality.

The room was shrouded in a heavy silence, the lingering echo of the gunshot fading away. The ticking of an antique clock on the wall seemed to reverberate in the stillness.

Then, from behind a concealed door, Hassan emerged, his presence a sudden and enigmatic intrusion. His gaze remained locked on the lifeless body of Foster, his expression inscrutable. He stepped lightly, his footsteps barely making a sound on the darkened hardwood floor.

Hassan's smile, that unsettling and ambiguous grin, crept back onto his lips. He seemed to exude an aura of triumph and dominance as he approached the table where Foster's lifeless form lay. It was as if he had orchestrated this chilling finale with meticulous precision.

"There was no worm, Falcon," Hassan uttered, his voice carrying an eerie finality. He leaned closer to Foster's lifeless body, as if addressing a silent witness to their twisted game. "You thought you could outwit me, outmaneuver me, but you underestimated the depths of my cunning."

He paused, savoring the moment, relishing in the victory that had been so ruthlessly claimed. The room seemed to hold its breath, caught in the web of Hassan's malevolent charisma.

"Falcon," he whispered, his voice a soft, chilling hiss, "you were but a pawn in my grand design. A pawn who believed he could challenge the master of the game. But now, the game is over, and the victor stands alone in the gallery of the night."

With that, Hassan turned away from Foster's lifeless form and retreated through the hidden door, disappearing into the shadows from whence he had emerged. The room remained silent, save for the soft hum of the television, as the enigmatic Hassan vanished, leaving behind only the haunting echoes of his malevolent triumph.

INSPIRATION FOR THE NOVEL SEAL - GHOST RECON

In the annals of television history, "A Question of Fear" remained an enduring masterpiece, a tale etched into the lore of Rod Serling's iconic series, "Night Gallery."

First broadcast on November 8, 1972, this chilling episode had transfixed viewers with its bone-chilling narrative. Theodore J. Flicker's teleplay, based on Bryan Lewis' story, had set the stage for an unforgettable experience. Guided by the deft hand of director Jack Laird, the episode had been brought to life by the formidable performances of Leslie Nielsen as Colonel Denny Malloy and Fritz Weaver as Dr. Mazi.

THE ORIGINAL PLOT

At a private club, the gentlemanly Dr. Mazi (Fritz Weaver) regales the men in the room with a story about a terrifying night he spent in an abandoned house, reputed to be haunted, adding that afterward he was committed to a mental institution for three years.

One brash guest, Colonel Denny Malloy (Leslie Nielsen, in his earlier tough-guy persona, a characterization similar to the one he portrayed two years later on *M*A*S*H** as Colonel (again a Colonel) Buzz "The Ringbanger" Brighton), scoffs at Dr. Mazi's account, calling him a coward.

Colonel Malloy, wearing an eyepatch and mustache, is a longtime soldier-for-hire and boasts that he is incapable of fear. Dr. Mazi makes him a $15,000 bet that he can't spend one whole night in that house without being frightened to death. Malloy gladly accepts the bet, laughing that "for $15,000, I would spend a night in hell."

At dusk one evening, Mazi's limousine drops off Malloy, carrying a backpack for his night's say, at the house. The front door opens itself, Malloy enters cautiously, and it shuts itself behind him. Immediately, the chills begin.

He hears a man's voice laughing/moaning. He sees a large spider in a web. Blood drips from above him onto his hand. A weird image of a disembodied head, in a yellowish/greenish light appears, floating around and there is more laughing and moaning.

Moving on to the dining room, Malloy finds a long table set for dinner, but crawling with rats. The flashlight he has with him dies and takes a candelabra for illumination, then walks out of the room. The candelabra remaining on the table blows out as he leaves and there is more cackling from an unseen voice.

He turns on a backup flashlight and a man, fully engulfed in flames appears. Malloy shoots at it with his revolver and it disappears. More blood drips onto the floor.

Malloy enters the basement, begins to descend the stairs and the door above him shuts on his own and locks behind him. A step breaks and he falls to the bottom where he is greeted with more maniacal laughter and sobbing.

He then enters a room and the voice becomes louder, as if it source is within. A ghostly man appears, charges him, and he shoots at it until his gun's chamber is empty. The man then disappears.

Malloy notices more droplets of blood on the floor, near where he shot at the spectral man. Heavily breathing and sweating, he escapes this area and finds a quiet place to take a break of hot coffee from his thermos along with a cigarette. It should be noted here that this is a long, extended rollercoaster ride of fear, largely without dialogue and excellently directed by series producer Jack Laird.

The sounds of a piano disturbs his silent break and he follow the sounds, opens a door and finds a male mannequin playing. The mannequin turns around and its hands burst into flames. Noticing a power cord, Malloy cuts it and the mannequin falls over.

Feeling confident, he addresses Mazi and the two others from the club aloud, saying they'll "have to do better than that."

He goes upstairs to bed, checks the bed and all seems ok although he notices a power cord under the bed which he severs. He staggers as he removes his boots, suggesting he may be drugged. Once relaxed and in bed, steel restraints suddenly emerge and cover his chest, locking him in. Then a swinging razor-sharp swinging pendulum descends, moving closer and closer to his neck. Just short of slicing his throat, the pendulum stops. He yells out that the things Mazi wants to see him afraid. He then falls asleep.

The next morning, he's awakened by an alarm. The restraints and pendulum are gone. He goes downstairs and enters the kitchen where coffee is made and toast pops up. Mazi then appears on a two-way tv. Mazi admits he drugged Malloy's coffee thermos.

Mazi then explains that his father was in the Italian forces during World War II when Malloy captured him. He was a concert pianist. Malloy remembers. Mazi reminds Malloy that when his father could not provide the information Malloy sought, Malloy then poured gasoline over his hands and set them ablaze, reducing them to burned stumps. Mazi's father never played piano again.

Mazi swore revenge on his father's deathbed. A biochemist, Mazi says he injected Malloy with a serum that will transform him into an earthworm. His bones will break down. Malloy scoffs at this and Mazi suggests he go down to the cellar and look at his colleague who is already a form of slug. Malloy sees a slimy trail on the kitchen floor. Fearing his fate, Malloy declares "you still lose, Mazi!" and shoots himself to death.

On the television screen, Mazi calmly replies, "no, you lose. There is nothing in the cellar."

A great, chilling, scary segment of Night Gallery. If you want to see a scary one, see "A Question of Fear."

(Night Gallery story, "A Question of Fear" posted by David Juhl, 12/28/2013)

ORIGINAL CAST TRIBUTE

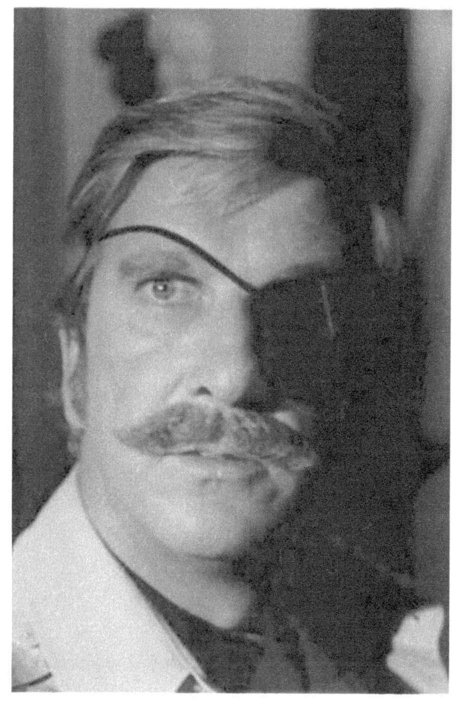

Leslie Nelson
Colonel Denny Malloy

Fritz Weaver

Dr. Mazi

TO MY READERS:

As the final chapter of "SEAL – Ghost Recon" comes to a close, I'd like to take a moment to express my gratitude to all you readers out there. Reviews are the lifeblood of any writer, offering insights into what resonated with you and what left you wanting more.

If you enjoyed this contemporary reimagination of "A Question of Fear" and found yourself immersed in the world of SEAL-Ghost Recon, please consider leaving a review on platforms like Amazon.com or Barnes and Noble.

Your thoughts and feedback are invaluable, guiding us toward new adventures and ensuring that our stories continue to haunt your imagination. Thank you for embarking on this journey with us, and may the shadows always hold a place in your heart.

What readers are saying about the author's other horror novels:

House on Haunted Hill Resurrection

5.0 out of 5 stars **Thrilling While I Read This Through A Thunderstorm!!!**
Reviewed in the United States on July 9, 2023

House on Haunted Hill is a captivating book that successfully delivers a sequel to the beloved 1959 movie starring Vincent Price. As a fan of the original film and a devoted admirer of Price's work, I had long awaited a worthy continuation of the story, and this book did not disappoint.

Reading House on Haunted Hill during a rain and thunderstorm added an extra layer of atmosphere, enhancing the chilling and suspenseful experience. The author's descriptive prowess allowed me to vividly imagine myself inside the mansion, feeling the same sense of unease and curiosity as the characters.

One of the book's greatest strengths lies in its ability to keep readers engaged from start to finish. Each page turn brings new twists and surprises, constantly leaving you guessing about what will happen next. The author skillfully weaves together elements of horror, mystery, and suspense, making it incredibly difficult to put the book down.

What truly impressed me was the seamless transition from the original movie to this sequel. The author successfully captures the essence of the 1959 film while injecting fresh ideas and expanding the story in a compelling way. It's evident that the author has a deep appreciation for the source material and has done justice to the original work.

House on Haunted Hill not only caters to fans of the original movie but also stands on its own as a thrilling and captivating read. Even if you haven't seen the 1959 film, this book can still be enjoyed for its strong storytelling, well-developed characters, and atmospheric setting.

Overall, House on Haunted Hill is an excellent read and a wonderful sequel to one of your favorite childhood movies. The author's ability to create a gripping narrative, coupled with great twists and an immersive setting, ensures that the book will keep you hooked until the very end. Whether you're a fan of the original film or simply enjoy a well-crafted suspenseful tale, this book is a must-read.

5.0 out of 5 stars **Genre Mastery Unleashed!**
Reviewed in the United States on August 25, 2023

In 'House on Haunted Hill: Resurrection,' the seamless fusion of horror, mystery, and suspense sets it apart as a true gem. The narrative takes you on an exhilarating rollercoaster of emotions, gripping the edge of your seat with each page turned. The twists and surprises that unfold are a testament to Rose's mastery of the genre, leaving me captivated and eagerly anticipating what's around the corner. In horror literature, 'House on Haunted Hill: Resurrection' stands tall, demonstrating Rose's prowess as a talented author. The homage to its predecessor while carving its path showcases Rose's ingenuity. With this captivating narrative, I'm eagerly looking forward to more from this author. A resounding bravo for a job well done!

Beneath the Earth

"Beneath the Earth" masterfully treads the line between horror and science fiction, offering readers an exhilarating dive into a subterranean nightmare. Set in the eerie remoteness of Russia, the narrative brilliantly combines the thrill of scientific exploration with the terror of the unknown. Gary J. Rose employs his knack for vivid and immersive storytelling, painting spine-chilling scenarios of scientists pitted against grotesque, acid-spewing spiders in the heart of the Kola Superdeep Borehole. The book's atmosphere of mounting suspense, accentuated by unexpected plot twists and the relentless drive for survival, ensures a heart-racing experience from start to finish. The narrative's underlying commentary on the potential hazards of toying with nature adds depth

to this thrilling spectacle. For those who appreciate the unique blend of science fiction and horror, "Beneath the Earth" promises a gripping, fear-inducing journey that will linger in your memory long after the final page.

5.0 out of 5 stars **Another Spine-chilling story you wont want to put down!**
Reviewed in the United States on July 29, 2023

After reading his book, House on Haunted Hill Resurrection, I couldn't wait for his next horror book to come out. You will not be disappointed and hoping for more from him.

As an avid reader, I definitely rate Beneath the Earth" as a 5-star read!! It's an absolute gem blending the best of horror and sci-fi genres into an adrenaline pumping masterpiece. The plot is like a rollercoaster ride full of fear and excitement, with the Arctic Storm and huge gigantic spiders creating an atmosphere of relentless tension. The authors' vivid words will paint terrifying scenes that will haunt your imagination even after you finish the book. The brilliant characters he developed show how their struggles and camaraderie resonate deeply. The relentless action and all the twists and turns will keep you guessing and hooked from the first page to the last. "Beneath the Earth" is an unforgettable, captivating experience. I can't recommend it enough for anyone seeking a spellbinding adventure. Another great read by Author Gary J Rose. Can't wait for the next one!

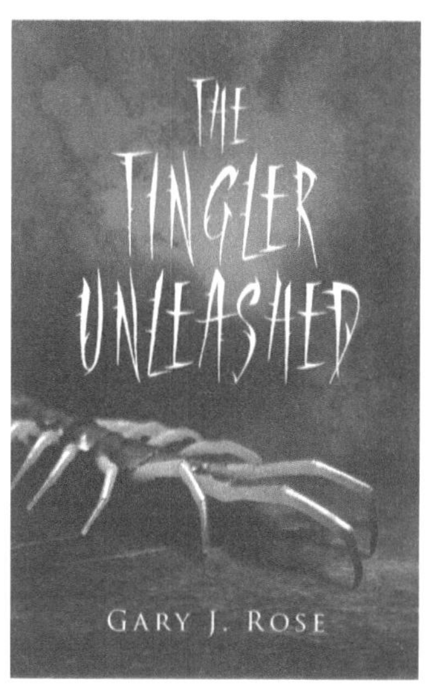

The Tingler Unleashed

5.0 out of 5 stars **Full of Unexpected Twists. So good!**
Reviewed in the United States on September 20, 2023

As a devoted fan of the 1959 classic, "The Tingler," starring Vincent Price, I eagerly picked up "The Tingler Unleashed," a reimagination of the novel that takes place six decades after the original film. This book brilliantly captures the essence of the cult classic while introducing a fresh and thrilling narrative. It's a delightful return to the spine-tingling world of Dr. Warren Chapin and his terrifying discovery.

The author's vivid descriptions and character development pay homage to the original film, making it a nostalgic journey for fans like me. However, it also stands on its own as a gripping horror tale that explores the legacy of fear and the consequences of tampering with the unknown. "The Tingler Unleashed" is a must-read for both longtime enthusiasts of the film and newcomers seeking a pulse-pounding, cinematic reading experience. It resurrects the tingling sensation of the original and leaves readers eagerly anticipating more.

5.0 out of 5 stars **A must-read for**
Reviewed in the United States on August 26, 2023

The Tingler Unleashed is a suspenseful, action-packed thriller with well-developed characters and a perfect blend of horror and comedy. I highly recommend it to fans of the genre. Gary Rose does an excellent job of updating the classic 1959 film The Tingler for a modern audience. The book is full of suspense, scares, and humor. Rose's writing is vivid and atmospheric, and he creates a sense of dread and unease that will stay with you long after you finish the book. The characters in The Tingler Unleashed are well-developed and relatable. You will find yourself rooting for them as they try to survive the Tingler. The plot is fast-paced and action-packed, and it is sure to keep you on the edge of your seat from beginning to end. Overall, I thought The Tingler Unleashed was an excellent book. It was a suspenseful, action-packed thriller with well-developed characters and a perfect blend of horror and comedy. I highly recommend it to fans of the genre.

COMING SOON

Carnival of Lost Souls

Highly decorated Detective Mary Holloway leaves the chaotic city life behind, seeking solace in the quaint seaside town of Safe Haven. But destiny takes a sinister turn when a fateful accident plunges her into the depths of a mysterious river.

Days later, Mary awakens on a desolate sandbar, her past life a blur. Determined to embrace her fresh start, she soon uncovers the town's chilling secret—a forsaken carnival grounds where people have vanished for a quarter-century. Now, Mary must confront the enigma of Safe Haven's Carnival of Lost Souls, a place where the living and the dead are forever bound by malevolent forces.

In this contemporary reimagining of the classic 1962 horror film, prepare to be enthralled and terrified as Mary delves into a nightmarish world where escape seems impossible. Will she unravel the carnival's mysteries, or become another lost soul trapped in its malevolent embrace?

www.ingramcontent.com/pod-product-compliance
Lightning Source LLC
Chambersburg PA
CBHW020548310726
48979CB00008B/1135/J